He was a man

Whitney grabbed a
your measurements

She nearly knocked him off balance by spinning him around. When she knelt in front of him, totally inappropriate fantasies took flight. Man, it was hot in this store.

He looked around, wishing there was an easy way to get out of this measuring gig, wishing he could shrug out of this sweltering jacket—when Whitney's palm cupped his tush. She tugged at the seat of his pants. He cleared his throat, wishing like crazy that her face wasn't at eye level with his zipper. She glanced up at him.

"Problem?" she asked. Her right hand went right up the inside of his thigh, all the way to the top, where she paused longer than both of them knew was necessary.

Images flipped through his mind of their one night together, so sharp, so clear, it could have happened just yesterday rather than three months ago.

"What are you doing?"

"Determining your inseam."

"Woman, that sass is going to get you in trouble."

Dear Reader,

"You don't own a tux shop for forty years and not know something about romance." So says Karl Delaney...and he's about to prove it for three bachelor buddies who have the fortune to rent from his shop. These three friends are about to get some BIG surprises!

Mindy Neff kicks off the DELANEY'S GROOMS series with *Suddenly a Daddy*. Originally from Louisiana, Mindy settled in Southern California, where she married and raised five kids. Family, friends, writing and reading are her passions. When not writing, Mindy's ideal getaway is a good book, hot sun and a chair at the water's edge. You can write her at P.O. Box 2704-262, Huntington Beach, CA 92647.

In the next two months, be sure to look out for *The Last Two Bachelors* by Linda Randall Wisdom and *Cowboy in a Tux* by Mary Anne Wilson, as DELANEY'S GROOMS continues!

Happy reading!

Debra Matteucci
Senior Editor & Editorial Coordinator
Harlequin Books
300 East 42nd Street
New York, NY 10017

Suddenly a Daddy

MINDY NEFF

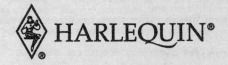

HARLEQUIN®

TORONTO • NEW YORK • LONDON
AMSTERDAM • PARIS • SYDNEY • HAMBURG
STOCKHOLM • ATHENS • TOKYO • MILAN • MADRID
PRAGUE • WARSAW • BUDAPEST • AUCKLAND

To my editor, Denise O'Sullivan,
with sincere appreciation for the opportunities
you've given me, your steadfast support from the
very beginning, and for your gracious, classy ways.

Thanks a bunch!

ISBN 0-373-16769-5

SUDDENLY A DADDY

Chapter One

He'd been having dreams about Whitney again. Hot, sexy dreams.

That had never happened in the past. She was his best friend, had been since they were kids—well, since Whitney was a kid anyway. But even though she'd been five years his junior, he'd never viewed the spunky young girl as a pest. They'd grown up together, formed a bond. He could always count on Whitney to keep up with him—more often than not she could outdo him—whether it was a competitive game of one-on-one or, like idiots, speeding down the coast highway in a sports car, playing chicken on the switchback curves of the cliff road or squabbling over a friendly round of poker or pool.

Whitney Emerson was game for just about anything.

She'd been his best buddy when he was seventeen…she still was fifteen years later.

So why the erotic dreams?

Probably because of the merger he was on the verge of agreeing to.

God, he didn't want to think about that now. He just wanted to unwind with a friend. Someone he could count on. And though he didn't see Whitney on a daily basis, or even monthly for that matter, the knowledge that he could count on her was a given.

With the top down on the Porsche and an eye on the rearview mirror for highway patrolmen, he barreled up U.S. 101, counting the cows that dotted the rolling grass-covered hills to his right.

"Angus, I keep going," he said out loud. "Hereford I stop." Cattle seemed a safer bet than flipping a coin, seeing as how he was doing a ground-skimming eighty-seven.

He tugged at the knot of his silk tie, inhaled the scent of sea air as a balmy January breeze ruffled his hair. That was the cool thing about California weather. You could have a heat wave in the middle of winter. And he loved it, loved the warmth brushing his face, especially when his insides had felt so damned cold lately. He pressed harder on the accelerator. There was nothing like driving too fast in a convertible, defying the law and testing his skills.

Not that he had a death wish or anything. He was restless. And he needed somebody. Somebody who wouldn't expect anything from him, wouldn't insist he make a decision or sign a check. Somebody who wasn't counting on him to line up backers for some cause or the other. Somebody who wasn't thrusting profit and loss statements under his nose, expecting him to perform a miracle or soothe a worry. Somebody who wasn't a project manager or programmer or lawyer or accountant or bank official or socialite hinting that she needed an escort to the opera.

Somebody like Whitney Emerson.

"Ah, to hell with the cows." His decision made, he whipped off the freeway and picked up State

Highway 1, doing a passable imitation of Mario Andretti as he raced along the coastal road, then into the heart of Montgomery Beach with its quaint boutiques, tree-lined streets and upscale galleries—the town named after his ancestor.

There was no way he could pass this close to Whitney without calling or stopping in. Tonight he needed to see her, needed to rest in the steady presence of a really good friend, someone he could just be himself with.

He pulled the Porsche up in front of a Spanish-style structure, deciding right then and there that the parking space at the curb was an omen. Usually he'd have to circle the block three times and still not get this close.

Expansive, arched windows faced the main street of town, their panes so sparkling clean he could see inside the store and clear through to the courtyard beyond.

He shut off the engine, slipped his Ray-Bans into the center console, picked up the cell phone and punched in a familiar number.

"Delaney's Tux Shop, how may I help you?"

"You could buy me a beer and a pizza."

There was a split instant of silence, then, "Dylan Montgomery! Where are you?"

God, he loved that excitement in her voice. No matter what, he could always count on Whitney to make him feel special. "Look out the window, darlin'."

He saw her gaze jerk up, saw her eyes narrow, saw that hand flick up to rest on her hip as though she were truly aggravated. Her smile stretched wide.

"Get in here, you turkey. And it's your turn to buy the beer."

He grinned, pushed the End button on the cell phone, then vaulted over the side of the convertible, pocketing the keys as he jogged the few steps to the door.

Karl Delaney, Whitney's uncle, owned this block square of town. A master tailor to stars, dignitaries and presidents, he'd settled in Montgomery Beach when Whitney's parents and sister had been killed in a plane crash. Karl hadn't thought twice about packing up his life and relocating to avoid uprooting his grieving niece.

He still kept a shop in San Francisco, but he'd bought this section of prime real estate and turned it into a bridal square.

The plaza was an ingenious idea. All the necessary shops built around a three-hundred-year-old oak tree in the center of a courtyard. Actually, what Karl Delaney had done was bridge the mission church that sat at one end of the block with the hotel that rested at the other.

One-stop wedding block. Shop for bridal gowns, tuxedos, sport clothes for the honeymoon, dishes, flowers, cakes, diamonds or stationery. Arrange vacations with the travel agent or buy your first home though the real estate company. Then marry at the mission church and spend a night or two at the elegant hotel with its steps leading down to the surf and sand.

And at the center of the hub was Delaney's, and Karl Delaney in particular. Whitney liked to tell people that there were Irish skeletons in her uncle Karl's closet, when in truth, the name had resulted from an overburdened immigration official with a bad case of writer's cramp who'd shortened Delaninstekhov to Delaney.

It was a well-known fact that Karl had a penchant for passing out advice—whether you needed it or not—usually in the form of a discreet note tucked into a suit jacket or the pants' pocket of a rented tuxedo.

Kind of like a fortune cookie, Russian style.

Whether it concerned grooms, randy kids headed for the prom or the country's highest officials, Karl Delaney had opinions and was more than determined to get them across.

Even the most hard-hearted bachelor or bachelorette couldn't help but feel a touch of romance when they happened upon this square.

Maybe that was why Dylan's heart was beating a little faster as he stepped though the door of the tux shop.

Or maybe it was the way Whitney looked when she skipped out from behind the mahogany counter like an excited schoolgirl.

Except she didn't come anywhere close to resembling a schoolgirl.

Dylan came to an abrupt halt and nearly swallowed his tongue. She wore a lavender camisole top and a clingy skirt that hugged and skimmed her body like a lover's caress. Though the fabric appeared opaque, its peek-a-boo illusion was guaranteed to heat a man's blood.

Before he could gather his wits, remind himself that this was Whitney he was having such sexy thoughts about—his best *friend*—she launched herself into his arms.

He caught her automatically, twirled with her, and just that simply, felt at home. At last.

The lump in his throat surprised him. He swallowed, hugged her and lowered her to the floor.

"Oh, Dylan, I'm so glad you're home. For how long? What's going on?"

"Hey, Slim, slow down."

"Well, it's been—what?—three months since you've been home. My gosh, there's volumes we need to catch up on. How long can you stay?"

"I'm just passing through." He couldn't stop himself from eyeing her silky ensemble again. He whistled. "That's some outfit."

Her smile rivaled the sun as she pirouetted for him. "Like it? I've been experimenting with fabrics."

His brows rose. "Nightgown fabrics?"

"Oh, you." She playfully smacked his arm. "If you're only passing through, what are you doing here?"

"I've just sat through three days of dreary meetings, and played an even duller round of golf over in Pismo. So I was driving back up the coast, playing that silly eeny-meany-miney-moe game with the black cows versus the brown and I thought, 'Dylan, my man, you need to liven up your crummy mood.' And naturally your face and name came to mind."

Her laughter kissed the walls of the men's shop like a sensual caress. "That's me, lively Whitney."

More lively than usual, he thought, and stuffed his hands into his pockets so he wouldn't reach out and touch. What was wrong with him? "What do you say? Want to grab a quick bite before I have to get back on the road?"

"You're not driving back to San Francisco tonight, are you?"

"That was the plan."

She shook her head. "You work too hard. What about your mom? She'll be upset if you're this close and don't stop in to see her."

A knot formed in his stomach. He hadn't been back to the estate much since his dad had passed away. Randolph Dylan Montgomery Sr. had been an autocratic son of a gun. People naturally fell in line and did what he ordered.

Funny, they were all still living their lives somewhat the same, even though dear old dad now resided over in Dillard's cemetery where a huge, ostentatious marble headstone marked his final piece of turf.

Sometimes Dylan felt as if his dad was still running things from the grave. It was as though his ghost still reigned, orchestrating everyone's lives.

The proposed merger he'd been approached with was one example.

"Hey." Whitney waved a hand in front of his face. "Where did you go?"

"Just thinking about Mom." Well, in a way, he had been. Randolph hadn't made her life a bed of roses, either. "You know, if you don't tell her I was here, there won't be a problem."

"Ah," drawled a masculine voice hinting at Russian roots, "but what if *I* should tell, young man?"

Dylan smiled and turned toward the impeccably dressed man whose blue eyes sparkled with joyous, mischievous light. Over six feet tall, slim and still attractive at sixty-two, Karl Delaney could never be described as overbearing. Dylan had so often as a boy wished that this man were his father. He had the understanding and patience that any kid would envy, the kind of understanding a certain rich kid had longed for.

Dylan held out his hand. "Aw, Karl. You don't want to get Mom mad at me, do you?"

Karl warmly returned the handshake, all the while scrutinizing Dylan's suit pants, silk blend shirt and loosened tie, giving a slight, unconscious nod of approval. It was a habit.

"And what of *my* ear blistering should she find out you were in my place of business? God knows the woman is a saint, but I certainly do not want to be in her line of sight when she is displeased."

His mother, barely five-two, could definitely tear a figurative strip off someone's hide if she put her mind to it. Oh, not in the way his father had. Grace Montgomery tempered everything she said and did with the utmost charm and love.

"Come on, Uncle Karl, keep our secret," Whitney pleaded, joining the game. "Besides, I haven't had a chance to tell Dylan about my trip to Paris."

Karl sighed, but the corner of his precisely trimmed gray mustache twitched. "Yes, of course. I have been struck blind today, can scarcely tell a pink Van Heusen from a crisp white Geoffrey Beene." He turned slightly and fussed with a stack of ivory-embossed stationery.

"You must both go and have a nice dinner—even though *someone* in town is bound to recognize and mention seeing that flashy Porsche and reporting in to—"

"Uncle Karl?"

"Yes, my dove?"

"You're pushing it." She grabbed a lacy cardigan from behind the counter and pulled it on.

He chuckled. "Go."

After placing a quick peck on her uncle's cheek, Whitney slipped her arm though Dylan's and ushered him out of the store. "So what are you in the mood for?"

"Something simple. I just need to unwind."

"Hank's place okay?"

Imported beer, the best and messiest barbecue sandwiches in Central California, the current sports game on fifty-two-inch TV screens and pool tables that only cost a quarter for a rack of balls. "Perfect."

"Walk or drive?"

"How about we drive to your place and leave the car."

"Sure." Hank's was only a block from Whitney's house. Even though the evening was turning chilly, he felt like stretching his legs. Besides, in Montgomery Beach, with parking harder to come by than hen's teeth, it made sense to walk.

As they drove the five blocks to Whitney's house, Dylan absorbed the familiarity around him. It was a great town, full of atmosphere and money. He couldn't think of anyplace else where the forest seemed to flow into the sea. One minute you'd think you were in the middle of a quaint mountain village, surrounded by chalets and tall, thick cypress, and then you'd walk a block and be on a white sand beach or a cliff overlooking lava formations frothy with the splash of sea spray. It was the best of both worlds.

Whitney's happy laughter drew his attention and he felt his lips curve. She did that a lot, just laughed from the sheer joy of life. Wind whipped her deep mahogany hair and, using both hands, she gathered the flyaway strands into a makeshift ponytail. In pure masculine reflex, his eyes lowered, just a bare fraction of an inch, a measure he sorely regretted. The lift of her arm caused her sweater to shift and her body-hugging camisole to cling even tighter.

Everything within him came to a heart-jolting halt.

"Watch the pedestrians!" she yelled.

He slammed on the brakes and snapped his gaze back to the narrow road. And by God, that's where it would stay, too. "Sorry. Guess I really do need to unwind. I don't normally mow down the neighbors."

"That's because you don't *have* neighbors around that mausoleum you live in." She pressed a hand to her chest, took a breath to steady herself.

"You're just jealous because I have more rooms than you do."

She rolled her eyes, shoved the sleeves of her skimpy sweater up to her elbows. "I don't have a jealous bone in my body."

"Such a tough girl. You've grown into a heart-breaker, Slim."

"Better to give than to receive, they say."

His laughter, spontaneous and unrestrained, burst out at her unintentional double entendre.

She whipped around, gave him a mock glare. "I meant *heartbreak* you idiot. And I'm twenty-seven, Dylan. I grew up a long time ago."

And how. He pulled the Porsche into her driveway and shut off the engine. It was a two-bedroom bungalow, with lots of glass and wood tucked back from the street. Though it was actually in the heart of town, it had the feel of privacy with its huge redwoods and oaks interspersed with fragrant cypress. In a couple of months flowers would bloom in the beds along the raised porch and sprout at will at the base of the many trees.

He'd helped her move in just a couple of years ago—a backbreaking experience he didn't want to go through again. Whitney could be very agreeable, but she had an artist's temperament, and that meant that everything had to be just so. And to get it "just so" he'd had to move every blessed stick of furniture at least twice, invariably ending up putting it right back in its original spot.

"What's that smile for?" Whitney asked, getting out of the car.

"Memories."

"Mmm. We've got a few of those. Which one in particular?"

"Moving day."

She hooked her hand through his arm and started them off down the sidewalk. "Oh, don't start on that. You'd have rearranged your furniture, too."

"No, I wouldn't. That's the decorator's job."

"Spoken like a true blue blood. Not everybody has an obscene amount of money like you do to throw around."

He felt his gut clench, dismissed it. "The way I heard it, you're close to catching up."

"With your bank account? Hardly."

"Don't be such a pessimist, Whit. Going to Paris? Studying with the big boys? That's got to mean big bucks for your future."

"*Future* being the operative word. Right now my bank account's more along the lines of ready-made-off-the-discount-rack. Someday soon, though, I'm gonna be bigger than Armani and Versace—and have the bucks to prove it.''

He smiled, slung an arm about her shoulders and steered her up the steps of Hank's. The smell of barbecue had his mouth watering. ''That's what I love about you, Slim. You know your mind and there's no swaying you once you go after a goal.''

''You realize, of course, you could be describing yourself?''

''Two peas in a pod, your uncle used to say.'' He tried like hell not to notice the sway of her hips in the slinky, body-hugging skirt as she preceded him through the door.

A damn near impossible feat.

Hank's was a place where the locals went. Whitney knew everybody and greeted them by name. On the way to a corner booth, she shouted across the room to the bartender. ''Coronas, Larry. Times two.'' She indicated Dylan with a wave of her hand.

Larry slung the white bar towel over his shoulder. ''Good to see you, Dylan.''

''Hey, man. Can't come into town without some of your great barbecue.''

''You both want the specials?''

''In a bit,'' Whitney answered. ''We'll start with the beer. And don't forget the limes.'' A long-neck bottle of beer wasn't complete without a wedge of lime, she was fond of saying.

Heads turned and conversations pulled up short as she moved across the room. Every man present shared a look of pure masculine appreciation. Whitney Emerson was a riveting presence with sexy attitude to spare. She lit up a room like a burst of skyrockets on a hot summer's eve, creating a roomful of male fantasies that were nearly palpable.

The hell of it was, she didn't even realize the effect she had on people—particularly men. If he'd pointed it out to her, she'd have looked genuinely baffled, then laughed and told him he was obviously stressed and half out of his mind.

She peeled out of her sweater, then scooted into a booth for two that rested on a raised platform at the fringes of the pool tables.

Dylan's gaze stalled right there at chest level. He made himself look away. "Sure you don't need the sweater?"

"Not if I'm gonna whip your butt in a game of pool."

He slid in next to her, wondering what had gotten into him. Maybe it hadn't been such a good idea to call her, after all. Clearly he needed to tend to his social life more. All work and no play was causing his brain to short circuit.

And to conjure fantasies about Whitney.

As soon as the waitress brought the drinks, he snatched up the bottle and took a healthy swig.

Whitney was watching a couple of guys shoot pool. Dylan felt the table shaking and for a minute he thought it might be an aftershock from one of the many California earthquakes. Then he remembered just who he was with. When she was either nervous or excited, or simply had a lot on her mind, Whitney's foot would get to bouncing about a hundred taps a minute. She did it without thought.

The bowl of chips on the table jumped like a tiddlywink and the flame of the candle did a hula dance.

Dylan reached over and placed his palm on her knee, an action he'd done a hundred times in the past.

The jolt was unmistakable.

This didn't feel anything like it had in the past. This felt brand-new.

Her head whipped around. He could have sworn he saw heat flair in those striking green eyes. A rosy hue crept up her neck, flushed her cheeks. Her lips parted.

Then she broke the moment by laughing and taking a swig of beer. "I've obviously got some excess energy here. How about a game?"

"Damn good idea," he muttered.

"What?"

"Sure." *Get a grip, man.* "We playing for stakes?"

"Does a squirrel have a bushy tail? Of course we are. Did you think you'd gone away and come back to a different girl?"

As a matter of fact, yes. Either that, or he'd come back a different man. "Getting cocky, Whit? You know I can take you with one hand tied behind my back."

"You wish. The bet's twenty for the game. And same as always, every time you scratch, you owe me a foot massage."

"Those massages are starting to add up."

"Yeah, and your tally's getting pretty high." She racked the balls, rearranged the stripes and solids. "If I didn't know better, I'd think you were staying out of town just to welsh on the bets."

He narrowed his eyes. "Now wait just a minute. Whose marker is getting high? Seems you scratched last game."

"Once. You did it three times, then skipped town. Do you want to break?"

"Ladies first."

She grinned. "You're such a gentleman, Montgomery. And you still owe me."

"Yeah, yeah. I'll pay up." He waggled his eyebrows. "Unless you want to go for double or nothing?"

"I'm gonna be a rich woman with happy toes. I can already feel 'em tingling."

At that moment, when she leaned over the table with the cue stick lined up and aimed at the triangle of colored orbs, more than just Dylan's toes were tingling.

The beer bottle suspended midway to his mouth as his gaze riveted on the outline of her fanny. The soft, clingy material of her long skirt was not pantyline friendly and, by God, if she was wearing a stitch of undergarment beneath that slip of fabric, he'd swallow that cue ball whole. Then again, she could be wearing a g-string or something.

That image didn't do a thing to cool him down.

Hell on fire, what was he doing obsessing over Whitney Emerson's underwear—or lack thereof? Disgusted with himself, he shook his head and brought the bottle to his lips.

With a loud crack that nearly made him jump out of his skin—and spilled beer down the front of his silk-blend shirt and tie—Whitney's break shot sent balls scattering across the table's green felt surface. A couple went in the pockets. For the life of him, he didn't know if they were stripes or solids.

She eyed the napkin he was blotting his tie with, her green eyes dancing with amusement.

"Miss your mouth there, Montgomery?"

"Cute." Vowing to pay better attention—to the game, *not* to Whitney's butt—he signaled the waitress for two more beers, and watched as Whitney neatly banked the five ball into the side pocket. Since he didn't think she was giving him an edge by knocking his balls in, he figured he was stripes.

"So, how's your love life?"

This time his mouth was empty so he didn't give away his jolt by spewing liquid. "Pretty nonexistent, thanks. And yours?"

She laughed. "The same. I've been so busy I haven't had time to think about relationships."

"No more calls from Devil?"

"Devlin," she corrected, giving him a squinty-eyed look that said she knew he'd mangled the name on purpose. "And yes, he quit calling. I have a feeling Uncle Karl slipped one of his famous notes of advice into Dev's pocket."

"Good. He wasn't right for you, anyway. There's something fishy about a guy who seems to forget his wallet every time he goes out with a woman."

She moved around the table, giving way so he could make his shot, and patted him on the cheek. "I told you I was only dating him for his looks. And speaking of looks, how about you and Suzy-Q?"

She was leaning against the felt-top table, right in his way. He raised a brow and tried to ignore the way his heart stuttered at the sexy, flirty look she aimed at him. His throat went dry and he took another swig of beer.

"Suzanne gave up on me when I stood her up for the opera." The thirteen spun like crazy and slammed right in, setting up his next shot perfectly. "Twice."

"Oh, Dylan, you *forgot?* That's rotten."

"Yeah. I think I'm getting old. I can't seem to remember my own name lately." He sighted the ball, then paused, his brows winging down. Whitney was leaning over the other end of the table, eyeing the lineup of his next shot. At any other time, on any other night, he'd have appreciated her interest and sportsmanship, the camaraderie of two evenly match opponents judging the skill, angle and spin needed to make a shot.

But just then, one of her little spaghetti straps slipped off her shoulder, giving him a tantalizing glimpse of cleavage. He gritted his teeth. "Do you mind?"

She glanced up at him with a flicker of surprise that cleared in a bare instant. Her smile was slow and sexy, her eyes widened in innocence. "Am I distracting you?"

"You know damned well you are." *Innocence my foot.* Buddy or not, he was still a man. And she was a hell of an attractive woman.

"Sorry. And, Dylan?"

He sighed, held up on his shot. "Yeah?"

"Don't be so hard on yourself. Thirty-two is far from senility."

"Thank you. Now if you'll just move aside, I'll try to make this shot before I'm *ninety*-two."

She did move. But her image was still burned on his mind. He missed the shot.

She grinned. "Oh, too bad."

"Brat." Two could play, he decided. Taking a cooling swig of beer, he set the bottle aside, then moved up behind her, crowding her, brushing lightly against her backside from waist to knees.

She jolted and shot straight up like a puppet whose strings had just been jerked. "What the heck are you doing?" She jabbed an elbow in his gut.

With an "oomph" he stepped back. He liked that breathy catch in her voice. At least, it sounded breathy to him. He was feeling a pretty good buzz from the alcohol. Like him, she blew a shot any kindergartner could have made.

"That was your fault," she accused.

"You started it." He chalked his cue stick, then stepped around her and judged his next move. With Whitney, there was no room for gentlemanly behavior in a hot and heavy game of pool. If he admitted to a foul and gave her an extra turn, she'd clear the table without blinking an eye. And by damn, he didn't mind giving that foot massage, but he was in the mood to receive, too.

She gave him room, leaning a hip against their booth, swigging beer and munching on chips, watching every move he made.

And damn it all, he sank the cue ball.

Her auburn brow rose as she sauntered toward him, her lips arranged in a pout that was supposed to appear sympathetic. And Dylan couldn't help himself. He laughed, hauled her up into his arms and, with her feet dangling off the floor, twirled her around.

Her breath caught and the cue stick slipped out of her fingers. With her hands on his shoulders for balance, she pushed her upper body back and looked at him. "What in the world has gotten into you?"

"I've missed you, Slim."

"Yes, well...uh, I've missed you, too."

"No. I mean it. I've *really* missed you. You can always make me laugh. You don't cater to me or my ego. You don't let me win. You make me *remember* to laugh."

He lowered her to her feet. She leaned over to retrieve the cue stick, keeping an eye on him as if she wasn't totally convinced of his sanity.

"Business getting to you?" she asked.

"Yeah. Finances are a little sketchy right now— but there's a merger pending. It's big, Whit. Really big. My computer chips married to laser technology." He gave an inward wince at his choice of words. Granted a marriage *had* been discussed, but he'd declined. "The medical industry is clamoring for it."

"Medical? You mean, like those wrinkle-erasing lasers?"

"Among others. Optical. Dental. I know just how to make them better than the rest."

She nodded. "You always were sharper than the next guy. Craziest thing, though. You don't look the slightest bit like an egghead."

He grinned and winked. "I left my plastic pocket liner in the car. Karl would have had a coronary."

Her laughter drew the attention and smiles of several patrons. "You've got that right." She laid a hand on his chest, gave a gentle pat. Her green eyes radiated sincerity and something else he couldn't quite pinpoint. Or maybe he was just reading emotions where there were none.

"I hope it works out for you, Dylan. It'll be a new direction to go in, something all yours...not your dad's."

Yes, she really did understand him. "I'm crazy about you, you know that, don't you?"

"Sure. I'm crazy about you, too." Her gaze clung for just an instant, then she crossed her eyes and gave him a goofy look before leaning over the table. The cue ball shot to the far rail then sailed back, splitting side-by-side balls and sinking them into the corner pockets.

"Nice shot."

"Naturally. You're not the only one who's good."

"My mistake. Lucky I've got you here to remind me. So, you never did tell me how it went in Paris."

"Wonderful. It's such a romantic city—even though I didn't get to see much of it. The design classes were intense and didn't leave room for sightseeing."

"That's a crying shame, Whit. We'll have to plan another trip sometime and fix that—at least get you to the top of the Eiffel Tower." He eyed the shot she was lining up. "So, what trade secrets did you learn on this intensive working trip? The latest in elegant gowns?"

She practically laid on the table, gently kissed the two ball, making a sweet side pocket. "Nope. We concentrated on sports."

"Sports?" He leaned on his cue, figuring the game was already over. She'd darn near cleared the table. "Now, there's a new one on me. Since when does fashion design correlate to football and stuff?"

"I didn't say football." She tapped her stick on the left corner pocket. "Eight ball, left corner. We learned about sport-*shopping* and sport-*lunching* and sport-*flirting*."

"Well *I* could've taught you that and saved you a bundle."

"Mmm, but could you have gotten me an exclusive audience with Galliano?"

"Dior's designer?" Whitney had told him before she'd gone that Galliano was her target. It didn't surprise him a bit that she'd attained her goal. "Impressive."

"Yep." The eight sank perfectly with a clunk. She straightened, held out her hand and gave a sassy grin. "Twenty bucks. Pay up, Montgomery. And don't even think about driving home tonight. You're gonna make good on those massages."

That's what he'd been afraid she'd say. And with this strange hum of electricity running between them all night—at least on his part—he wasn't sure it was such a good idea to touch any part of Whitney Emerson's bare skin.

He'd never had a foot fetish, but the way his system was short circuiting, he just might end up developing one—with his best friend.

Chapter Two

Whitney took a bracing breath of cool night air, inhaling the scent of sea and forest. Crickets sang and a breeze ruffled the leaves overhead.

"Good thing we walked," she said with a slight giggle. "I think I'm sort of tipsy." As if to prove her words, she stumbled over the uneven sidewalk.

Dylan's arm shot out and wrapped around her waist. Chills raced up her spine, dotted her arm. She'd always reacted to Dylan—even though she'd never let on to him—but tonight the sensations were magnified. And he was acting different, too. Was it the alcohol? They'd drank a heck of a lot more than this in the past and never acted as if the next fiery look was going to ignite into passion.

And she was probably reading his signals all wrong.

"Step on a crack, break your mother's back." The childhood singsong made her laugh. It also made it impossible to walk like a normal person. Once the silly idea was planted, she would not—*could* not—step on a crack.

"That's bad, Whit."

"I know. And I apologize to your mother."

His smile flashed, that indulgent look he'd been giving her since they were teens. Her stomach flipped and she nearly tripped up again. This time with her heart—an organ that wasn't as tough as Dylan had earlier intimated.

To steady herself, she held on to his arm as they walked down the sidewalk, the streetlights shining pools of light in their path. A night bird whistled several piercing notes as though scolding them for disturbing his rest.

"How come you wear those platform shoes? Don't they kill your feet?"

"No. They're super comfortable. And they're in fashion."

He snorted. "You've never given a fig about what's timely, and you know it. You were always the one to set the trends."

"So maybe I like the way they look with this skirt, the way they make my legs look. That last beer made 'em a little unstable is all."

"The shoes or the legs?"

"Both."

"Well, dangerous or not, I agree. Your legs look great."

She bumped her shoulder against his. "I like you, Dylan Montgomery. How come we never dated?"

She felt his stillness, even though they continued to walk. What had possessed her to ask such an explosive question?

Finally he shrugged, the warmth of his arm brushing hers. "I guess because we've always been buddies."

"You're right. No sense in muddying up a good

thing with sex." They'd reached her house and she
inserted the key in the front door and pushed it open.

"Now, hold on just a minute, Slim. I never said
anything about sex being muddy. Though it's been
so long, I might be glamorizing it."

She laughed, feeling pleasantly light-headed and
uninhibited. She turned and dropped her forehead
against his chest, clutched his tie in her fist and gave
it a tug.

They'd stood just like this countless times before.
So why was there a sudden hush, a shift in mood, a
crackle in the atmosphere?

Her palm flattened against his chest. She felt his
heartbeat thud beneath her hand, change. Slowly she
pulled back, raised her head. Her platform heels
boosted her up close to six feet—the perfect height
to look him right in the eye.

To kiss him.

His gaze was focused on her mouth. Suddenly the
house took on an intimate air that had never been
present before. It was surprising, thrilling, scary.

She sucked in a breath. "Dylan?" she whispered,
puzzled. "What is this?"

"Damned if I know."

His voice was low and rough, a temptation the
most devout saint couldn't have resisted. She felt his
breath against her lips, wasn't sure which one of
them made the first move. Anticipation drummed in
her ears, beat in her pulse.

"It feels like I have a fever," he murmured. His
lips pressed against her eyelids, her brow, her temple.
Both hands tenderly cupped her cheeks, his thumbs
tilting her chin up just so, the perfect angle for a
lover's kiss. "God, Whit, I know we can't, we

shouldn't—but I have to…'' His mouth closed over hers, sampled, nibbled.

She tasted his heat, his reluctance. She grabbed his tie again. Something that felt this right couldn't be wrong. "Can't's not in my vocabulary." With a tug on silk, she urged him fully inside the house and backed toward the sofa.

A twinge of unease intruded for just an instant. Both their defenses were down; she might be taking advantage of the moment, of Dylan. A nagging voice poked at her conscience, hinting that she ought to tell him what this really meant to her.

But then his tongue did something incredibly clever to her ear at the exact instant his hands skimmed her sides, grazing her breasts. Every noble thought vanished in a puff of sensual smoke.

Need made her desperate as she shoved aside plump pillows, swatches of fabric and paper patterns strewn on nearly every available surface. A mannequin draped with butterscotch rayon watched from a shadowy corner of the room. Moon glow streamed in the plate-glass window and skylight, giving the room light without having to flick on a lamp.

That was fine. Whitney could negotiate by feel, was powered by sensation.

And those sensations were making her wild with impatience.

She tugged his tie again, tore at his buttons, jerked the hem of his shirt from his pants.

And his hands were busy, too, helping, unsnapping, shedding, his lips never once relinquishing their hold on hers. His Italian loafer landed on her coffee table with a clunk. She felt his mouth curve against hers, heard him swear as he jerked at his shirt and nearly strangled himself with his tie.

He pulled back, just a bit. "We've got to slow down."

"No." She was afraid if they slowed down, one of them would come to their senses. And she'd waited way too long for this night, was finally feeling bold enough to pursue it, to pursue him, to satisfy her fantasies.

To at last make love with Dylan Montgomery.

Her Dylan.

She put her hands on his bare chest and nearly groaned at the heat, at the flex of skin and honed muscle.

"This outfit's been driving me nuts all night." His left palm swept from the back of her thigh clear up her spine. His other hand pressed firmly against the small of her back, holding her in place, sandwiching her right up against his body in a way that both frightened and thrilled.

The want was huge. She'd never felt this throbbing, these sensations, never knew this was what it was all about.

"Lift your arms." He inched the hem of her camisole up, his thumbs brushing the underside of her sensitive breasts. He groaned. "I knew it. There's no room for anything else under this fabric."

She helped him get the top off, never gave a thought to the delicate fabric that went sailing across the room, felt a giggle build when she noticed that it landed right over the top of the mannequin. Then the giggle died before it even had a chance to work its way up her esophagus when his thumbs hooked in her skirt, lowered it, explored the silky lines of her nearly nonexistent panties.

"You are a man's most cherished fantasy."

The words washed over her like a caress. And when he lowered her to the sofa cushions, she forgot that this was her best friend, the guy who'd taught her to drive a car, taught her to smoke and then to quit, the guy who was with her the first time she'd gotten drunk.

He was her dream man, the man she'd waited a lifetime for...even though she hadn't truly realized that until tonight.

"It's been so long, Whit. I'm not sure if I can go slow this time."

This time. She wasn't going to let herself even begin to think about a possible next time. She just wanted now, right now, this minute.

"Then don't." She opened for him, urged him over her, dug her fingers into his sides. "I want you, Dylan. Now." She could hardly get the words out. Her breath came in pants, and she nearly screamed when he reached down, tested her readiness, lingered to tease, to torture, to send her right over the edge.

She whimpered, might have begged.

With her legs wrapped around him, she pushed against him. "Please..."

"Wait."

"No."

"You make me crazy," he said, and thrust into her.

It was like a bucket of ice water tossed in her face. This time her scream wasn't one of pleasure.

"What the hell?" He started to withdraw.

She grabbed his hips, wrapped her legs tighter. "Just give me a minute." The shock was subsiding.

"Man alive, Whit, why didn't you tell me?"

"Just shut up, Dylan." The pleasure was seeping back in, pooling in her belly, fluttering her insides, raising gooseflesh on her skin. She pressed her lips to his shoulder, nipped his earlobe, and lifted her hips against him. "Just shut up and make love to me."

For a long, humming moment he simply looked at her. Then, at last, he complied. Only this time his movements were much slower, his touch much gentler. And all the while he continued to watch her in a way that made her squirm. She closed her eyes. That nerve-pulsing sensation was building again, and she wasn't sure she wanted such close scrutiny if it spiraled anywhere close to where it had been before that sobering first thrust.

Now, though, she felt him, hot and heavy inside her. Felt a friction that sent chills of pleasure so strong she didn't know if she could breathe. She prayed that she could be cool about this, that she wouldn't make a fool out of herself if the mind-numbing stimulation overwhelmed.

And she'd just as soon he not watch her so closely.

She felt his hand between them, felt his thumb stroking in a way that brought her right to the brink of madness. Her eyes flew open.

His velvet-brown gaze was still on her. Intently.

Curiosity and pure sensory images took over, transporting her to a place where there was only touch and feel and pleasure. To hell with what he was seeing. She slammed her eyes shut, moved against him, with him, let the tide build, cascade up and reach for the peak.

Tears burned at the backs of her lids. She held her breath, wanted this feeling to last all night, a lifetime, just like this...oh, just like this.

And then, against all reason, the pleasure built even higher.

"Look at me, Whit."

Her nails dug into his shoulders. She shook her head, squeezed her eyes tighter as ribbons of vivid color danced and spun.

His body went still. She nearly screamed in frustration.

"Look at me," he repeated.

She did. Anything to keep the momentum, to reach the goal. She wanted to know what it was. "Do it, Dylan. It's so close. It almost hurts. I never knew..."

"I know." Eyes locked, he began to move, slowly, then faster, creating a tempo that burst through her blood and pounded in her heart.

She felt the building crescendo, was almost afraid of its power.

"Stay with me, baby. That's it. Let it go. Don't fight it."

She grabbed the back of his neck, jerked his mouth to hers, ate at his lips as that final wave teetered then crashed in a glorious flow of power and light and sensation. A flow that drowned out sight and thought and reality. A flow that narrowed her world to just her and Dylan, to the scent of them, the feel of them, the utter rightness of it all.

She felt reborn, weak as a kitten yet powerful enough to shout from the highest mountain.

"Wow," she muttered.

Dylan didn't respond. He rolled off her, sat up and reached for his pants. "I think we better talk."

Uh-oh. Here it comes. Reality. She wished to heaven it hadn't come so quickly, that she'd had just a few more minutes to revel in the sensations.

There was guilt on his face, though, lurking in his eyes.

Regret.

She could see it clearly without the benefit of a light, feel it in the vibrations of his tone, vibrations that stung her heart like tiny pricks of a fine-gauge needle.

Damn. The lump in her throat threatened to give away her emotions, and that was unacceptable. She wouldn't put pressure on Dylan, would do just about anything to erase that regret on his face, to hide the fact that what had happened between them had been a life-altering experience, one she'd longed for since she'd first learned at fifteen what those tingly feelings meant.

She pasted a smile on her face, gave a flippant pitch to her voice. "Well, I don't know about you, but I'm pretty worn-out and still a little light-headed from those beers." *Yeah right.* She'd sobered up the second his mouth had closed over hers. The corners of her lips trembled. "But if you insist, let me just get a robe."

Dylan watched her walk out of the room. She had an incredible body, an athlete's body, strong and toned. He groaned and pulled on his pants. He'd never in his wildest dreams imagined this happening tonight—well, maybe in those wild dreams. Still, he was sure there were rules between them. His blood was still pumping so fast and hot, he couldn't think of them.

This couldn't have happened at a worse time. He

felt like a cad—especially after that last business meeting he'd attended. The tentative terms of that merger made what just happened between him and Whitney all the more inappropriate.

She'd been a virgin, to boot. He'd just deflowered his best friend.

She came back in the room, flipping on lights. Her pale green robe looked cloud-soft and enveloped her like a full-length winter coat, hiding all those incredibly sexy, womanly parts that had gotten him in trouble in the first place.

She hooked a wrist on her hip. "Honestly, Dylan, there's no need to look as though you've been caught stealing the crown jewels."

"That's about the way I feel. You were a virgin, Slim."

She shrugged. "So. It's pretty archaic to be that way at my age."

"Why me?"

Again her shoulder hitched. "Why not you?"

An uncomfortable silence hummed between them. "This changes everything," he said quietly.

She couldn't abide that regret in his tone. "Are you kidding?"

His head jerked up, his eyes narrowing.

She trudged ahead. "We're friends, Dylan. Nothing has to change between us."

"How the hell can you say that?"

"Oh, come on. You're getting all worked up over nothing. So what if I'd never actually done the deed before. It's no big deal."

His brow shifted. "Great. Now she attacks my ego."

She laughed. "I didn't mean it that way. You were

great, buddy. But you have your life and I have mine—goals that are really important to each of us. You've got your laser merger to pursue, and I've got a name to make for myself in the fashion industry. Think about it. We don't need the hassle of trying to turn a lifelong friendship into something more.''

''Who said it would be a hassle?''

''Wouldn't it?'' she asked softly. ''We didn't plan this, Dylan. No sense making more out of it than is really there.''

She picked up a pin cushion that had rolled under the end table, set it next to the cloth tape measure coiled atop a swatch of crimson polyester.

''What if there *could* be more?''

She crossed her arms and looked out the plate-glass window at the moon shining overhead, the stars winking in the velvet sky.

''I'm not willing to take the chance to find out. I'm moving toward a goal in my life that might well take me out of the country.''

She turned, looked at him. ''I couldn't bear it if I lost your friendship, Dylan, if trying to make our relationship *more* ended up messing up the closeness we already have.'' Tonight had been impulse. She needed time, time to see how he acted, if there was something that could truly grow. Because she couldn't lose again. Not Dylan. He'd been there for her when she was a girl broken by the loss of her parents. He was a constant in her life. It was imperative that she let him go tonight, to absolve him from any regret or guilt. Because if their impulse made him feel noble—and that nobility wouldn't stand up to the light of day—she wouldn't be able to bear it.

She pushed her hair behind her ear, took in a

breath. "You were the one who introduced me to just about every other first in my life, Dylan. It feels right that you should have been the first to show me about sex, too. Let's don't make more out of it than is necessary. Consider what we did tonight as furthering my education."

"Your education?" He came to his feet, jammed his arms through the sleeves of his shirt but didn't bother to tuck it in.

He still felt poleaxed over what making love with her had made him feel. Emotions swirled, strange and new, unlike anything in his experience. He didn't know how to define what he felt, didn't know if he really was placing too much importance on them, as she was trying to tell him.

But furthering her education? It ticked him off that she could be so flippant about the whole thing. That wasn't the Whitney he knew.

"There's no need to get dressed, Dylan."

With a shoe in his hand, he paused. "Why? Thinking of going another round for education's sake?"

He knew her temper could flash. He should have been prepared for the thimble that came sailing across the room and glanced off his shoulder. Reflexes quicker, he ducked the package of chalk that followed, then moved across the room and grabbed her by the shoulders before she could get a hold of something sharp and more dangerous.

"I'm sorry, Slim. That remark was uncalled for."

"You bet it was. Remind me not to go drinking with you anymore."

He sighed, rested his forehead against hers. "I guess you just dented my ego."

"I meant it as a compliment."

"Yeah, I know." They stood just like that for a long time. "Sure you don't want to see where this could go?"

"Timing's wrong."

He brushed his thumb over the tiny scar above her lip. The result of a rogue wave knocking her off her feet and into the lava rocks. He'd had to take her to get a stitch. She'd balked and given him grief the whole way.

He smiled. "You're a tough cookie, Whit."

"I learned from the best." She put a finger over his lips. "And don't get huffy again. I meant that in the best possible way."

Just that gentle touch sent his stomach into a flip. He shook his head. Crazy. Whitney was his buddy, his confidant, his calm, steady port in every storm.

The reminder felt hollow and hypocritical. Tonight he'd taken things way beyond friendship.

And he'd held back confiding in her—something he'd never done.

She was letting him off the hook, but he still felt a twinge of guilt. If he came clean, though, he had an idea that busy careers or not, she'd probably throw something a lot more dangerous than a tin thimble or box of chalk.

"I should go."

"Tonight? It's late."

"Not that late." So why did it feel *too* late? And for what? "I'll make good time without the traffic."

He bent to kiss her cheek just as she shifted her head. Their lips brushed.

They both sprang apart like naughty children.

He chuckled even though his blood was pumping. "This really could get complicated, you know."

"Not unless we let it." As though to prove that it was no big deal, she went up on tiptoe and brushed his lips again. "Have a safe trip, buddy. And if my number's not the first one you dial next time you breeze into town, you're in deep trouble."

"My knees are shaking."

Chapter Three

Whitney was sipping peppermint tea when she got the frantic call from Leena's Bridal.

"Whitney, you've got to come. It's a rush, we need alterations within a week! I can't believe she's left it so late—but it's a good family and all. Be a dear and squeeze this in for me?"

"Right this minute, Leena?"

"Yes! Just look out the window if you doubt. She's up on the fitting pedestal now and…" A long-suffering sigh, a rustling sound. "Oh, it pains me."

Though nausea still churned in her stomach, Whitney smiled. "Don't go getting in a dither. I'll be right over."

"Hurry. The girl is determined to leave straight away!"

Whitney shook her head. She could see Cori Spencer through the glass panes since Leena's Bridal was directly across the courtyard from Delaney's Tux Shop. It was both convenient and a little tricky. On more than one occasion, a bride had been having a fitting at the same time as her groom was being measured for a tuxedo. And Uncle Karl fully believed in that bad luck thing about a groom seeing his bride in her wedding gown before the ceremony. He was such a romantic.

"I'll be right back, Uncle Karl. Leena's got an emergency."

Karl looked up from checking the shoulder seams on a blue pinstripe the advertising executive was trying on. The man had wanted flashy. Appalled, Karl had talked him into conservative, certain the man wouldn't seriously want to call undue attention to a body that had been underexercised and overindulged. The blue—conservative, correct and streamlined— would minimize flaws and just might pull off the illusion of suave. One could certainly hope.

He watched his niece walk out the door and skirt the stone planter that protected the grandfather oak. His discerning eye noted the slight droop to her shoulders, though to others she would simply look like an elegant vision in pale celery, all flowing lines of lace and satin and sheer georgette. He'd always been a conservative man, but he had to admit that Whitney could pull off flamboyant avant-garde with flair.

The pallid hue of her cheeks, though, was a fairly good match to her green dress, and that worried him.

Some investigating and poking would be in order. He would not deem to advise lest he were certain of the facts. And once he had them, he would fix it, whatever *it* was.

Whitney pulled open the door of Leena's Bridal, and smiled at the tiny woman all but wringing her hands in oh-so-subtle outrage.

"There you are, dear. We've but a moment or two to correct the fit and do my dress justice."

And a fine dress it was, with yards of satin and

hand-sewn beads and textured roses patterning the skirt so subtly it took a shift of lighting just to notice the exquisite detail.

It was a wonder Whitney even noticed at all with her preoccupation.

Spring was in bloom. And to Whitney's everlasting horror, so was she. Just the thought made her stomach churn even more.

Especially because she hadn't heard from Dylan since that night in January.

It was now April.

She shook off her thoughts, focused on the dainty blonde standing on the raised platform in bridal white, looking as jumpy and skittish as a cat trapped in a roomful of overflowing bathtubs.

Whitney couldn't help but smile.

"She would not even take the time to remove her clothing," Leena imparted, scandalized. "Something about a stake-out, just breezing in here, fitting us in between jobs!"

Whitney patted Leena's arm. "I'll take care of it." She knew Cori Spencer—living in a small town had its advantages. Cori was a detective with Montgomery Beach Police Department. Short hair, cute, but her looks were deceiving. She could take down a three-hundred-pound man without hardly breaking a sweat.

The handsome guy over there in the corner, looking both angry and uncomfortable that he'd been dragged into a bridal shop, was a puzzle, though.

The groom? Whitney wondered with a raised brow. Uncle Karl wouldn't approve.

"Well, Cori, this is a surprise." A quick lift of the voluminous skirt revealed just what Whitney had suspected. "This hem's gonna be a bit tricky unless you're planning on wearing combat boots down the aisle."

Cori shook her head, gave a soft laugh. "Just do whatever. The best you can is fine."

The dress definitely needed a few nips and tucks. "I'd like to do better than that. Hold your arms out." She took straight pins out of her wrist cushion. "I didn't even know you were planning to marry."

"We just made the decision a week ago. I wanted a quick thing, but mother had a fit. Said she wouldn't be cheated out of a society wedding, especially since she'd despaired of me ever getting married in the first place. And since *nobody* argues with my mother, I told her if she could pull off a fussy to-do in two weeks' time, I'd at least show up. Bobby can tell you—oh, have you met Bobby?"

"No."

"Well, then, Bobby, Whitney. Whitney, Detective Bobby McCullaugh." Quick and to the point. That was Cori.

"Nice to meet you," Whitney murmured around a mouthful of straight pins. Marking the bodice for another dart, she glanced at the antsy male officer, wondering how he felt about a splashy but rushed wedding. She was about to ask when a pager started beeping.

Several women in the shop checked their purses. Cori's partner checked his belt. But if Whitney wasn't mistaken, the annoying signal was coming from inside the folds of the wedding gown.

Sure enough, Cori reached down, swept up the hem—thank goodness she was wearing her pants, after all—and pressed the button. "Gotta go."

Whitney quickly drew chalk lines, stuck in another pin, all while Cori was stepping impatiently down off the fitting pedestal.

"Undo these buttons, Bobby," Cori demanded, bending to tug off the crinoline. Not only was the woman wearing her jeans, she hadn't taken off her T-shirt, either. Whitney made another hasty chalk line, then stepped back for fear that somebody would get hurt in all this haste.

Bobby hesitated. Cori glanced back, frowned. "Any time today would be fine, partner."

Detective Bobby McCullaugh swore and flicked tiny buttons that ran down the back of the gown.

"I wish you'd let me get a better idea of the fit without those clothes beneath," Whitney complained. If she was going to do something, she hated to give it any less than her best.

"It'll be fine. My clothes are skintight anyway. Can't throw the measurements off too much."

"Yeah, well don't blame me if your ta-tas pop out because the bodice is too loose and saggy."

Bobby made a funny strangling noise.

Seeming oblivious to Bobby's discomfort, Cori laughed and stepped out of the dress, leaving it in a huge pool of satin on the floor.

"You're the best there is, Whitney, which gives me absolute confidence that my ta-tas will be perfectly respectable and in place." She tugged at her white T-shirt, tucked it back into her jeans, then clipped on her shoulder holster—the only concession she'd made to undressing. Heading toward the door, she shoved her arms into the sleeves of a blue Windbreaker that had the Montgomery Beach Police Department initials emblazoned in white across the back. "Hey, I just had a thought. Are you seeing anyone right now?"

Dylan's face swam into Whitney's mind. "No. I'm way too busy."

"And that's not healthy. You're looking pale, my friend, and I've got just the guy to put a little color into those great cheeks of yours. Come to our engagement party tonight. The best man's a dish. You've got to meet him."

Probably another police detective with testosterone to spare. "No thanks, I'm—"

"Please. Promise me. It's right next door at the hotel. Terrace Room, seven-thirty. Mother's having a coronary because the seating is uneven. Boy, girl, boy, girl, boy, boy. Horrifying! And you know these snooty to-dos aren't my thing. Be there, Whitney, and bring Karl with you. The more *real,* down-to-earth people I have around me, the better I'll feel. I'm counting on you." She dashed out the door her partner was holding open.

Whitney watched Bobby McCullaugh put a protective hand at Cori's back, and felt a pang of envy. Ridiculous.

So what the heck? Maybe she ought to go meet this dish of a best man and get a free meal, to boot.

Besides, she needed something to get her mind off her own dilemma.

Of how to tell her best friend that he was going to be a father.

THE GREAT THING about a one-stop wedding square was that you didn't have to go far for any or all of your needs—including entertainment and parties. It was especially convenient for Whitney since the hotel was only a courtyard's distance away.

The sea air was chilly, but the scents and rhythmic sound of the surf were so familiar, so comforting. Whitney tucked her hand into Uncle Karl's arm, using him to steady her steps on the uneven cobbled pavers. The splash of a lighted fountain vied with the roar of the sea just beyond the buildings. All white stucco and adobe red, the Spanish architecture was a subtle clever blend of old and new.

"I have not had tuxedo orders from the detective squad," Karl commented as he pulled open the hotel's heavy glass doors. "Are you certain of the parties involved in this wedding?"

"Fairly certain." She patted his arm. "Don't worry. They wouldn't dare order tuxedos from anybody but us."

The hotel lobby was lit by a chandelier dripping tear-drop crystals, its massive span eye-catching and awesome. There had been upgrades here, but the renovators Uncle Karl had hired hadn't sacrificed authenticity for modernization.

A sweeping staircase with carved cherry banisters and maroon floral carpet runners curved to an open terrace room above. It didn't take much of an imagination to picture gaily dressed women with painted lips and rouged cheeks leaning over the railing, beckoning beaus or sailors on leave to come up.

Floor vases the size of a small child stood along the walls, filled with fresh flowers that drenched the room in sweet scent. Mirrors tracked one's every move, giving ample opportunity for vanity gazes or for quickly checking exposed slips or mussed hair.

Whitney lifted the hem of her long emerald skirt

as they started up the stairs. Karl's hand covered her fingers where they rested on his arm, gave a squeeze.

"You are feeling up to this?"

She glanced at him, nearly missed her step. "Yes, why do you ask?" He was so observant. And she didn't want him worrying about her.

"Just inquiring. You know I am a worrier, and you have been off your food these last days."

Her burst of laughter echoed off the ruby-flocked walls. "You make me sound like a horse or some kind of animal off his feed."

Karl looked properly scandalized. Often he didn't understand teasing. He'd been in the country since nineteen fifty-two, but he had yet to shed his native Russian accent, or his correct bearing. "I would not call you an animal."

She patted his fingers. "Of course you wouldn't."

The room was buzzing with conversation and noise. China and crystal clinked against silver as hors d'oeuvres were passed around and consumed over cocktails. All around them was white linen and candlelight and understated opulence. A tasteful ensemble played soft tunes from the far corner and a couple of oldsters were taking a turn around the dance floor. Tuxedo-clad waiters wove silently through the guests, offering drinks and food, careful not to intrude or interrupt.

"Cori was right. Her mother seems to have a knack for last-minute shindigs. She's done a great job." Her gaze traveled around the room, searching out the guest of honor and her groom.

She saw Cori by the head table, an elongated linen-draped rectangle among a sea of round seating.

But it wasn't the table placement and style that made Whitney sway.

Her jaw dropped and nausea churned, rising up to lodge in her throat. Her heart pounded like a drum in her ears, rushing like the sea, swamping her, buzzing, making her dizzy.

Oh, God, she was going to faint. Right here in front of a roomful of expensively clad engagement party guests. A white haze narrowed her field of vision as silver specks flashed like pinpricks of mercury in front of her eyes.

Karl's elbow tightened against her arm, his fingers squeezed her hand. Not by a single wince did he reveal that he was aware of her nails digging into his flesh even through the charcoal rayon silk of his suit sleeve.

"Shoulders square, my dove," Karl whispered.

Whitney made a conscious effort to shut her mouth, to find that backbone Uncle Karl was reminding her to draw on. Though she still leaned into him for support, she stretched her lips into a smile, her gaze frozen on the man whose dark, familiar head was bent close to Cori Spencer's, his arm around the woman's trim waist.

"Is he...did you know, Uncle Karl?" Her voice trembled, was barely a whisper.

"No. Gracie has been preoccupied but she did not tell."

Even through the roaring in her ears Whitney was able to grasp that odd statement. Determined to stand on her own, to hide her shock, she took a small step away, breathed deep, squared her shoulders and looked at her uncle.

"You've been hanging out with Grace Montgomery?'' Dylan's mother, the woman who was even now seated at the head table.

The table reserved for the engaged couple's family.

Karl sniffed, put on that haughty expression that spoke of extreme displeasure and tugged at his sleeves. "I do not *hang out.*"

Whitney didn't have a chance to respond, because the din in the room suddenly dipped like a chorus of night insects going silent for a split instant when disturbed, then starting up again, a shift almost too subtle to grasp unless one was paying close attention.

And Whitney was paying very close attention.

She knew a lot of the guests in this room, knew at least half of the family members. That's what made her heart sink, what made her feel foolish for holding on to a shred of hope that all was not as it appeared.

And just then, Dylan Montgomery, her very best friend in all of the world, looked up, his expression transforming into one of profound shock and dismay.

She felt as though every one of the guests was covertly watching…waiting, like spectators who'd come to see a race but were secretly anticipating a gnarly crash.

But no one here knew what had gone on between her and Dylan three months ago. To them, Dylan and Whitney were friends. Nothing more. No reason in the world why anyone should look at her with pitying glances, or be searching for an adverse reaction. That was merely Whitney's fertile mind galloping off on the wrong pathway, like a wild mustang startled by a thunderclap.

And she *did* feel as though she'd been knocked askance by a vicious clap of thunder.

For the life of her, Whitney didn't know where she found the gumption to cock a brow at Dylan, to give him a sassy look and hint of a smile, to point to her own chin in a gentle indication that he should shut his slack jaw.

She imagined she could see that dimple in his right cheek crease ever so slightly, the way it usually did when he was on the verge of a smile. But of course they were standing too far apart for her to actually see the character trait.

That was the thing with Dylan, though. She didn't have to see stuff to know it was there. She knew him.

And as of three months ago, she knew a heck of a lot more.

Her face heated.

Karl tsked. "Do show some decorum."

She spared a glance for her uncle. "Excuse me?"

He searched her gaze like a parent reading truth or lie on a child's face, then heaved a sigh and shook his head. *"Nichivo."* Never mind. "It is as I thought."

She frowned, not understanding what he was talking about. Speaking in code wasn't normally Karl Delaney's style. Cryptic notes slipped into a pocket, yes, but verbal evasion, no. Rather than dwell or question, she let it go. Because right now her attention was still wrapped up in Dylan.

She saw him start to move her way, saw a distinguished older gentleman block his path.

"William Spencer," Karl said, nodding at the dapper man in gray tweed. A quality jacket, pricy, custom tailored. He could tell all that from a glance.

"Cori's father?"

"Yes. They reside in San Francisco, make their money in computers that have something to do with hospitals or medical."

Whitney's stomach did another odd flip that threatened ugly consequences if she didn't settle down. She remembered Dylan's words. *There's a merger pending. It's big, Whit. Really big. My computer chips married to laser technology.*

"We must decide, my dove, whether we intend to move out of the doorway or make a fast departure."

Whitney took a steadying breath. "I'm no coward, Uncle Karl. We'll move out of the doorway. Besides, there could be a really good reason why Dylan's at Cori Spencer's engagement party. And if not, then it's no big deal. It's not as if I have a claim on him or anything. We're just good friends."

Another look around the room revealed several of Montgomery Beach's police officers, as well as Detective Bobby McCullaugh whom she'd met earlier in the bridal shop. And again, Bobby was looking at Cori with that deep enigmatic expression that could have been annoyance or desperate, soul-touching love.

Karl opened his mouth to speak, then closed it again when Cori spotted them.

Whitney's penchant for searching out and finding silver linings crashed and burned when the other woman tugged at Dylan's sleeve and urged him across the room, straight toward Whitney and Karl.

Her face felt as though it would crack the way her lips were stretched in that frozen smile.

"Whitney! Thanks for coming. You're a peach! Meet my intended." She gave an odd chuckle. "This is Dylan Montgomery. One of *the* Montgomerys."

Whitney bit her lip, and raised a brow at Dylan, knowing that she would chew off her arm before she would ruin this night for either of them.

"I know. Careful how you pump up his ego, though. It doesn't take much and when it happens he's a bear to live with."

Cori's smile burst like the sun. "Oh, you two know each other! I should have realized."

"Whitney and I grew up together," Dylan said quietly.

"Then you'll have plenty to catch up on. Mother's looking like she's about to bust the seams of her girdle. I should go see about it before there's bloodshed or something. She's not thrilled that I invited half the police force, or about having to serve beer. Too common, you know." Cori grinned and turned. "Keep each other company while I go keep the peace—protect and serve and all that."

Dylan watched Cori make her way back across the room, her stride sure and confident. She wasn't a tall woman, but her innate confidence made her appear like a feminine giant. It was hard not to appreciate or like Cori Spencer. In so many ways, she reminded him of Whitney.

He turned, looked down at his friend. Karl had slipped away and it was just the two of them standing there. Or at least it felt that way, if such a thing were possible in a roomful of people.

He felt his stomach shift, felt his heartbeat speed up as he gazed at the woman who was watching his fiancée weave her way through the crowd. His emotions were all over the place and he wasn't sure what to do with them, how to feel, how to act.

Which was a first. He'd never had any trouble being himself around Whitney. Not Whitney, of all people. His best friend.

How could he define their friendship, though? Friendship seemed too generic a word for what they shared.

He knew she liked salsa on her salad and ranch dressing on her chips, that she drew stick people and fashion designs on every scrap of paper or cocktail napkin at her disposal, that she sneezed around cats but fed every stray within miles, that she'd walk over hot coals for family and friends, and that she hated her hips.

She'd encouraged him to go for it when he'd been toying with a new computer design, even though his controlling father had advised—even threatened— against it.

She'd slapped sticky notes in his pocket organizer when he took himself too seriously, seen him through several rocky relationships, always getting to the heart of the matter by asking him that crucial question: was he in love.

She could clear a pool table like a pro, drink him under the table, and loved to watch the sun rise and set.

She was his friend.

And she'd been his lover for one night.

And now she was looking at him with hurt in her eyes, a hurt that shamed him right down to his soul.

"I ought to knock you flat, Dylan Montgomery. I can't believe you didn't tell me you were getting married!"

Chapter Four

Dylan held his arms out from his sides. "Go ahead. Take your best shot."

She rolled her eyes, looked away. Though she kept up a brave front, he saw her hurt and disappointment. She flinched when he touched her cheek and he felt like a real jerk.

"I'm sorry, Slim."

Her shoulders lifted in a flippant shrug. "For what?"

"For not telling you about this."

"It's not as if you owe me anything."

"I owe you friendship, the courtesy of telling you important stuff so you don't have to find out this way."

"There is that. The shock alone could give a girl a heart attack."

He wondered if she was really that good at masking her emotions or if she truly was okay with his marriage plans.

He remembered their night together, how she'd told him their sojourn into intimacy was no big deal, that it didn't mean a thing, didn't affect their friendship, didn't alter anything.

He'd convinced himself that she was right, convinced himself that there were no real obstacles preventing him from accepting Spencer's terms for the merger.

Now that he saw Whitney, though, he was having a major conflict of emotions.

"Really, Dylan, it's fine…uh, wonderful that you're getting married. I was just surprised, is all. I mean, you've had plenty of relationships with other women. I've been there through every one of them. I guess it just never occurred to me that you'd make one of them permanent."

"Why?"

She looked at him oddly for a moment, then laughed softly. "Honestly? I have no idea. You've always been so driven, so…" She made a helpless gesture with her hands. "I don't know, so like a confirmed bachelor. Love 'em and leave 'em."

A wash of shame flooded him. The skin at the corners of her eyes pulled taut in a flicker of emotion that was gone so quickly he might have imagined it.

But they were both obviously thinking about the ramifications of that "love 'em and leave 'em" statement.

In essence, he'd done that with Whitney, too.

And for the crowning blow, he'd come back to town engaged to another woman.

She looked around the room. "Jack O'Connor's here?"

He followed her gaze. He and Jack had been fraternity brothers at Stanford, tight friends. Dylan was godfather to Jack's son, Patrick. "I asked him to be my best man."

She turned back to him. "By rights, I should be

your best man, Dylan.'' Then she laughed again, drawing smiles from several onlookers.

For some ridiculous reason, it bugged him that she could so easily offer to be in his wedding, that she could so easily accept that he was about to link his life through marriage to *another* woman.

Never mind that he was doing so with the equivalent of a gun to his head.

''Hey,'' she said, squeezing his arm. ''I was teasing. No need to get all worried and uncomfortable. I've never met Cori's parents before, but from what she's said they're high society all the way. They'd have a fit if you deviated that far from proper protocol—even though I have to say I do look pretty spiffy in a tuxedo.''

Whitney watched as he ran a finger around the collar of his pale marigold shirt, knocking his coordinating tie slightly askew. She automatically reached up to right it, and frowned when he nearly leaped back.

''Boy, are you jumpy.'' Odd that he hadn't even smiled at her remark about the tuxedo.

''Sorry. Keyed up, I guess. I just drove in a half hour ago.''

''Ah, that makes a difference.''

''For what?''

''For neglecting to tell me about Cori. I think I can forgive you since you've only been in town such a short time. Although there are these really nifty things called telephones, you know.''

He opened his mouth to say something, then took her arm and steered her to a table. ''Let's sit.''

''Before you embarrass us all by sprinting out the door?''

He smiled, and she realized it was the first genuine expression of relaxation she'd seen him give this evening.

"You know me inside and out."

"Anybody who'd care to look close enough could see you don't like these social shindigs. But you're a good sport, Dylan. You know when it's necessary to bite your cheeks and plaster on the charm."

"God, that sounds phony."

"Phony's okay on occasion. Seems a little odd that it would be necessary at your engagement party, though." Just saying it out loud gave her a punch in the stomach, a flutter that stung. She dismissed the discomfort.

Dylan signaled a waiter. "Want a drink?"

"Mineral water with lime will be fine." Her leg started to bounce, shaking the table. She made a conscious effort to stop.

He raised a brow. "Give up alcohol?"

"Just not in the mood." Whitney glanced away. She saw Uncle Karl doing his magic quarter trick with Jack O'Connor's son while Dylan's mother, Grace Montgomery, looked on with the rapt attention of a woman who adored children and magic.

Karl had an effect on people that made them shine and smile. With Karl and Grace Montgomery, though, there had always seemed to be just a little something extra. That extra spark.

Kind of like the extra spark between Whitney and Dylan.

"Jack's looking good," she commented. Dwelling on what she was drinking—or *not* drinking was dangerous territory.

"Yeah. Fatherhood suits him."

Whitney nearly choked on a pâté-smeared cracker. "I should hope so after five years," she said dryly. "If he wasn't a near pro at it, I'd be concerned. It's nice that he came for you, though."

"Actually, it's not just me he's here for. He came to look at property, too. He's thinking about relocating. Says he wants a slower pace, a better atmosphere and school system for Patrick."

Whitney glanced at the little boy whose white shirttail was wrinkled and didn't have a prayer of staying tucked into his pants. She'd never paid much attention to kids. Now she noticed them everywhere.

Deliberately, she set aside those thoughts. "You can't find a better place than here. He'll be happy."

As they'd done so many times in the past, they sat there at a corner table, allowing their gazes to cruise the room. They discussed people they knew, and speculated on the ones they didn't. It was their game. Catch up on news, pick one another's brains or create lives for strangers.

Tonight, there was a fine hum of strain between them that neither would acknowledge nor admit to.

And that strain nearly broke Whitney's heart. She took a sip of mineral water, wished that they could leave, knew that they couldn't—at least, not together as they could have done at one time not so long ago.

"Who's the guy with your sister?" she asked.

"Mark Forrester, my second in command and vice president of marketing. I've decided to open a branch of Montgomery Industries here in town. Mark's volunteered to scout locations and get things up and running. Plus, he's a groomsman in the wedding."

"Oh? I guess I haven't heard you talk about him much. Why is it that I didn't know who your second in command was?'' God, she was starting to get really picky. It seemed as though everything said between them tonight held the potential to hurt—served to show her that her smug belief that she knew everything about this man, knew him best, wasn't as accurate as she'd thought.

''Mark's only been with me about eight months.''

''Oh.'' *Ninny.* Since his father's death six months ago, she'd hardly seen Dylan.

''I was lucky to find him. He's a good guy, though he's a major workaholic.''

''Worse than you?''

''Much. But he seems to have his eye on Candice. So he's not too torn up about being here instead of San Francisco.''

''I'm surprised J.T.'s not here. Didn't you ask him to be in the wedding?'' Residing in Texas now, Whitney knew that J. T. Watson was also one of Dylan's closest friends. In college, Dylan, J.T. and Jack had been like the three musketeers. Whitney had spent countless hours listening to Dylan tell stories about the escapades of the three friends.

And heaven help any woman who innocently happened upon all three of these guys together. To a man they were handsome as sin, rich as Rockefeller and sexier than any heart-throb movie star. They were a potent combination and they knew it.

''I asked him,'' Dylan said. ''He put me off, said he had a commitment that weekend.''

''What's the frown for? That happens sometimes. I don't think he'd deliberately blow you off.''

Dylan shrugged. ''I'd hope not. Funny, though, he always asks about Candice when I talk to him, and then he gets this weird tone to his voice, backs off. Know what I mean?''

"No."

"It doesn't make sense. It's like something went on with those two." His shoulders lifted. "You'd probably know better than me. You and Candy are close."

True. There was a bond between Whitney and Dylan's sister, something that just felt...*more*. Hard to explain. "She's never said anything to me."

"Maybe I'm just reading something into it that's not there. Besides, I probably didn't sound real enthusiastic when I called, didn't make this thing sound important."

Odd how he kept referring to his engagement as "this thing."

This was a question she really didn't want to ask, but needed to. For friendship's sake at least.

"*Is* it important, Dylan?"

He was quiet for a long time. "Remember the merger I told you about?"

She nodded.

"Spencer's offering me a deal worth a billion dollars. It's something I've always been intrigued by—laser applications. Ever since I saw that light show at Disneyland when I was a teenager."

Images cast across the water's surface, she recalled, characters rising up to dance on the theme park pool—all controlled by computers and pinpoints of light. They'd seen it together.

He hadn't really answered her question with regard to Cori. Only with regard to business. For some reason, Whitney couldn't make herself press.

"I'd say you *are* reading more into J.T. not being

here. Usually people need a little more advance notice than a week to be in a wedding. Unless you've known longer?" Her stomach on the verge of taking a dive, she was relieved when he shook his head.

"No. Both Cori and I have busy schedules. When Spencer pushed, we thought to just go on down to the courthouse and take care of it. We both had the last weekend in April open so we penciled it in. Cori's mother had a cow and that's how we've ended up with bridal gowns and tuxedo rentals and attendants and churches and engagement parties."

She raised a brow. "I don't recall seeing any appointments for tuxedo fittings on my books. You better not be thinking of going to the competition."

His gaze skittered away for just an instant. Then he reached out and tweaked her hair. "Like I said. I haven't had much time to do anything, much less book appointments. Now that Jack and Mark are here, though, I imagine we'll be in tomorrow. Think you can squeeze us in?"

"Well, I don't know," she teased. "We're pretty sought after, you know. Just last week Arnold Schwarzenegger came in for a custom fitting."

"Caused the tourists to flock, huh?"

"Forget tourists. The locals were the ones drooling on the glass and eating all of Uncle Karl's candy." Everyone knew of Karl's sweet tooth and the fact that he kept candy dishes on every counter surface. A gutsy move, keeping chocolate around thousand-dollar shirts and jackets.

"So, how is The Terminator?"

Whitney grinned. "You sound jealous, Dylan."

A dimple creased his cheek. "Maybe I am." His

gaze traveled over her outfit. "You're looking pretty hot these days, Slim."

The compliment was offhand, very similar to the one he'd given her three months ago. But tonight they weren't drinking to excess. Then again, could she really blame that incident on alcohol?

"Remember you're an engaged man, buddy."

"So. Can't I comment on how my friend looks?" His gaze sharpened, and it was as though he was attempting to look inside her soul, to ferret out her secrets, to determine if she was telling the absolute truth—that she had meant it when she'd told him nothing between them would change.

God, she was developing an imagination!

"That one of your designs?"

She glanced down, forgetting for the moment what she was actually wearing. "Yes," she said absently. Her tailored short-sleeve shirt was a gossamer layer of sheer tulle delicately embroidered with petite buds in the palest celery green. Beneath the sheer fabric she wore an unlined shell that flirted with indecency yet shouted elegance. The scalloped hem rested below her waist, topping an emerald satin skirt that skimmed her ankles.

"You've got a lot of talent, Whitney. No wonder celebrities are flocking to the store."

She brought her attention back to the subject at hand. "I don't think Schwarzenegger's interested in my designs—"

"You mean to tell me you're not tinkering with men's designs, too?"

"Yes. No. I mean, yes, I'm doing men's stuff, too. What I meant was that I suspect our celebrities come in more for Uncle Karl's notes of advice. He's getting a reputation as the newest guru to the stars and dignitaries.''

''Still advising the president?''

''Oh, Lord, Dylan. He's *faxing* suggestions to the White House.''

''No!'' Dylan chuckled, pretending to be scandalized.

''Yes! I caught him at it just the other day. Can you imagine? A Russian immigrant advising on our international relations with Russia.''

''Well, he's in a good position to advise on that score, wouldn't you say?''

She rolled her eyes, then naturally turned her palm up when Dylan covered her hand with his. Her heart skipped a beat, then gave a deep thud that sent a rush of vertigo through her.

''So, barring a rush on celebrity fittings, suppose you'll be able to make time for me tomorrow?''

Funny how easily she'd forgotten why he was really here. She smiled, even though her heart felt like a lead weight in her chest. ''Sure. You know I'll always make time for you.'' She always had.

There was a commotion a couple of tables away, and Dylan and Whitney both turned. Cori's mother was fanning herself as though about to faint. Cori was tapping her foot impatiently, shoving her pager back into her bra—Whitney did a double take on that one—and signaling Bobby McCullaugh to her side.

Then Cori and Bobby were moving toward the table where Dylan and Whitney sat, and it wasn't until just then that Whitney realized how this must look. She was monopolizing the groom, off in a corner table, ignoring everyone else.

Guilt made her squirm and scoot her chair a little farther from Dylan's.

Cori, rather than acting miffed, actually smiled gaily when she breezed up to their table. "I've got a call, Dylan." She put her hand on his shoulder, then leaned down and brushed her lips against his cheek. Bobby McCullaugh stood like an impatient sentry behind her, looking at his watch.

"You're leaving?" Dylan asked.

"Yes. Duty calls. You understand, don't you?"

"Sure."

"You're a good guy, Dylan." Cori reached over and patted Whitney's hand. "Seems like I'm always running out on you. Take care of him for me?" She indicated Dylan with a nod of her head.

Dumbly, Whitney nodded, but she felt horrible. For a minute she was certain she was going to be sick. She'd been monopolizing Dylan half the evening, and the bride-to-be hadn't even batted an eye, didn't show an ounce of worry, had no idea of the depth of intimacy between them.

And now Cori was blithely turning Dylan over to her—giving her permission to play stand-in as guest of honor at the engagement party.

Oh, what a mess. Even if she'd been toying with telling Dylan her dilemma, she knew now that she couldn't.

Whitney truly liked Cori Spencer. She would not, could not, wreck this woman's life.

WHITNEY MADE IT TO WORK late the next morning. Standing at the counter, her elbow propped on the mahogany surface, she swallowed repeatedly, tried sipping tea, then gave up for fear that she'd embarrass herself. She needed a bed, needed to lie down, needed to get out of here.

Actually, nausea was the least of her problems. Dylan was expected to come in for a tux fitting.

She'd never dreaded anything so much in her life.

She'd tried to get out of it, claimed she couldn't make it in today, but Uncle Karl, the crafty old reprobate, had nixed every lame excuse she'd come up with. Not wanting to totally give herself away, she'd had to grab a figurative hold of her bootstraps and make herself walk the five blocks to the tux shop.

She fished a peppermint out of the crystal candy dish, popped it into her mouth, and nearly choked on it a minute later. Dylan walked into the shop, his godson Patrick perched on his shoulders. Jack O'Connor followed, and Mark Forrester brought up the rear. Lord have mercy, there ought to be a law against that much testosterone and sex appeal occupying a single space.

Just last night she'd been thinking that Dylan's friend, J. T. Watson, rounded out the sexy scale—and he certainly would have if he'd been here. But Mark Forrester wasn't chopped liver, either. Medium height, average build, a yuppie type in a nicely tailored three-piece suit. An all-American kind of guy who exuded masculinity and confidence that could catch a woman by surprise.

And Jack O'Connor. Well, Whitney had been privy to his brand of potency before, and was semi-prepared. The guy was melt-your-bones gorgeous, a millionaire and a shameless flirt. A lethal combination if ever there was one.

And then there was Dylan. Oh, God, why did those dimples have to cause her stomach to cartwheel like this? Why now? Had somebody slipped something in the water? Given her a weird hypnotic suggestion that caused her to go all fluttery and stupid every time she laid eyes on him? What had happened to good buddies? A punch on the arm, the ease to burp in front of him, the no worries if he saw her in her sweats with no makeup?

Now she found herself fluffing her hair, smoothing her blouse, touching her tummy, wondering if it were pooching. Wondering when babies started moving in their mother's womb. Wondering if all of a sudden her abdomen was going to distort and look like a gremlin trying to punch its way out of a Nerf ball.

She was going off the deep end here. Lord, when had she developed such a wild imagination?

Silently apologizing to her unborn baby for likening him or her to a gremlin, Whitney moved out from behind the counter and pasted a happy, welcoming smile on her face.

"Well, this is what we like to see. Four great-looking guys in need of formal wear."

Dylan lifted Patrick from his shoulders and set him on the floor. The five-year-old marched up to Whitney, looked up at her, his brown eyes twinkling with mischievous lights.

"Are you a mommy?"

Whitney nearly passed out. Blood rushed to her head, roared in her ears.

Jack chuckled and laid a hand on his son's shoulder. "Come on, sport, lighten up." To Whitney, he said, "Sorry, he's got a fixation about mothers lately."

Whitney finally got a grip on her emotions. For

one wild moment she'd thought this small boy had honed in on her condition and was about to spill all.

Hands trembling, she turned and reached for her tape measure. "Okay, which one of you would like to go first?"

"You are behind this morning, my dove," Karl said. "Mr. O'Connor and Mr. Forrester have already been in and I have made do. Mr. Forrester only needs to try on a jacket that I have right here." Karl held up the coat he'd draped over his arm.

"But you, of course, would not know this because you were tardy this morning." Cagily, Karl turned to Dylan. "I worry, you see, that she does not look so chipper first thing in the mornings these days. The dark circles, the stomach upset." He tsked.

"Uncle Karl!" Whitney was scandalized that he would discuss her looks or health in front of these men, men who were customers, never mind that she knew them, that one of them was Dylan.

That was even worse.

"Oh, I do apologize, Whitney."

She rolled her eyes, shot him a warning look—which he blithely ignored. What in the world was Uncle Karl up to? She didn't trust that particular twinkle in his blue eyes. His accent seemed a little more pronounced today, drawing out her name, giving it three distinct syllables. If she didn't know him so well, she'd be tempted to believe her own made-up stories, that there were Irish skeletons in his otherwise Russian closet.

Karl held out a hand to young Patrick, and the boy's chest puffed out like a little man's as he clasped palms with Uncle Karl and gave a hearty pump.

"May I show you our styles, sir?" Karl asked the boy, treating the five-year-old as though he were a very important customer in his own right, not just an extension of his monied father.

Patrick only hopped a little, then remembered himself and nodded his dark head solemnly. "Yep. I gotta look just like Dylan and my dad, though."

"I am certain we can accommodate you, young sir. I always say, a man who understands style and quality is far more likely to succeed."

"My dad's 'cessful," Patrick said proudly.

"Yes, and you will notice, I'm sure, that all of his suits are hand-sewn rather than fused. You must never, ever allow anyone to sell you a garment that has been fused."

Patrick frowned, thought about that for a moment, then nodded.

Karl hid a smile. He was a sucker for kids, would have loved grandchildren. Since he'd never married…well, that was a subject best left untouched.

"Now, if you gentlemen will follow me," Karl said, his gaze encompassing Jack, Mark and Patrick. "We will get you on your way. Whitney will take care of the groom."

The way he said "groom" caused Whitney's gaze to snap to his. But Uncle Karl had already turned his back and was retreating, accompanied by all but Dylan.

The moment she'd dreaded was here, and there was nothing she could do to get out of it. So she squared her shoulders, raked her gaze over Dylan from head to toe, mentally tallying his measurements, hoping to God she could pull this off.

Casually.

Without bursting into tears or jumping his bones.

Both were emotions she was fighting, and it was touch and go as to which one garnered the most importance.

"Okay, Dyl, are we going for traditional? Or tails and top hat? You want vintage? Trendy? What?"

His eyes crinkled at the corners. "What do you think?"

"Uh-uh. You're the customer. Besides, I know these things aren't really up to the groom. The bride usually determines the style."

"Present company's bride excepted," he said.

Whitney actually laughed, feeling calmer for some reason. "Yeah, I'd forgotten. A bride who can't even bother to take off her jeans to try on a gown is bound to not care a lot about detail. So, I'll rephrase. What has Mrs. Spencer dictated?"

"Traditional. Conservative." His head tilted ever so slightly and his gaze dropped to the floor. She'd seen that combination of gestures a million times in the past. She waited a beat. Then, wham, his eyes were back, pinning her, speaking to her, full of magic and mischief and charm.

Whitney gripped the mahogany counter because her knees had gone weak. That devilish smile of his was enough to knock a woman for a loop.

Her own lips curved up; she couldn't help it.

Her head was already swishing from side to side. "I know that look, Dylan Montgomery, and I'll not be party to what you're planning."

"Aw, come on, Slim. Just a little something wild. Shake up Ms. Spencer a bit."

"Young Ms. Spencer or old?"

"Old. Admit it. She needs a few less stays in that corset."

A giggle escaped. "What makes you think she wears a corset?"

"That bug-eyed look."

"You're bad."

"So, are you gonna abet or what?"

"Not when it comes to our tuxedos. Uncle Karl has a reputation to uphold, you know. Now, if you just happened to stop into Sole Attack by mistake—you know that trendy shoe store across town?—and picked up a pair of those red Creepers, Delaney's Tux Shop couldn't be held responsible for deviating from the rules."

"Those platform shoes? The shiny ones with the holes in top?"

"Those would be the ones."

"How about purple?"

"That'd work."

"Go with me?"

"No way!"

"Aw, come on. Be a pal."

She turned away, grabbed a tape measure. She wasn't feeling like a pal right now. Bones jumping was winning out over tears bursting.

"I'm gonna be a pal and get your measurements right. Though I'm not altogether certain why you're renting a tuxedo when you own several perfectly good ones."

He shrugged. "Just feels like the one for the wedding should be rented and returned. Otherwise, every time I went to the opera or a black tie affair, I'd feel like I was going to my own wedding again. It's weird enough that I'm doing that in the first place."

She paused, hope winging when she knew darn well it shouldn't. "If you're not sure, Dylan, now would be a good time to admit it and back out. You're talking about a lifetime commitment here."

Right before her eyes he seemed to age five years, looked incredibly tired, sad even. "I've given my word."

For some reason his statement canceled out any compassion she'd started to feel, and made her mad. Yes, Dylan was full of honor and integrity. Once he gave his word he wouldn't back down. But how much of this was due to his father's conditioning?

She'd often wondered if Randolph Montgomery's ghost wasn't floating around the corners, watching, poking, prodding, messing up, snapping an authoritative finger that everybody still jumped to.

The subject was way too touchy to get into now. "Fine, then. Let's get you in a tuxedo that fits."

She pulled the cloth tape measure from around her neck, feeling just ornery enough to give Dylan Montgomery something to think about besides his damned honor.

She led him to the fitting room, handed him a pair of pants, a jacket and a conservative white shirt with subtle pleats. "Try this one."

She chewed a nail waiting for him to dress and come out, planning her strategy. If what she had in mind didn't shake him up, then she didn't deserve the title of "woman."

When he stepped out of the dressing room, her heart stuttered and her bravado faltered.

She was the one all shook up.

Dylan Montgomery was a man born to wear a tux.

Chapter Five

The way she was looking at him when he came out of the changing room made Dylan pause—and check to see that his fly was zipped.

It was.

"I might have known," she muttered.

"What?"

"Nothing."

Dylan frowned when Whitney nearly knocked him off balance by spinning him around. He could usually second guess her actions and moves, but he was having trouble reading her mood right now.

And that made him nervous.

Especially since he kept noticing how that black leather miniskirt hugged her derriere and rode up on her thighs. She was wearing a pair of those platform heels again, which brought her right up to his height. Still, he had a few inches on her. And that put him at the distinct disadvantage of being able to look down her flirty, low-cut top.

Karl Delaney was known to indulge his niece's every whim, but clearly the man ought to put his foot down and implement a stricter dress code.

When she knelt in front of him, his tongue nearly

dropped to his shoes. Totally inappropriate fantasies took flight. He reeled them back in. Man, it was hot in this store.

He looked around, feeling on edge, wishing there was an easy way to get out of this measuring gig, wishing he could shrug out of this sweltering jacket, wishing Mark Forrester would quit pacing like an impatient workaholic, wishing Jack O'Connor would quit staring out the window looking as though he'd just swallowed a guppy—or seen an angel.

Before he could speculate further on his friends' behaviors, Whitney's palm cupped his tush. His gaze slammed down to the top of her head, and he was really sorry for the movement.

Those fantasies were still alive and well, and growing now that her hands were actually *on* him.

She tugged at the seat of his pants, jerked, nearly cut off his circulation…and she definitely shouldn't be pulling those pants so tight across the front like that. Otherwise she was gonna see more than she should.

Hell, every customer in the store was going to see more than they should.

He cleared his throat, wishing like crazy that her face wasn't at eye level with his zipper. She glanced up at him.

"Problem?" she asked.

"Could be." He sounded like a bullfrog. He *never* sounded like a bullfrog.

The imp actually grinned at him.

"I don't remember this particular ornery streak of yours." Sweat beaded at his hairline, trickled over his temples.

"Just goes to show you don't know me as well as you thought."

"I know you better than any other man does." Now his voice was soft, intimate. He didn't know why he baited her that way, why he suddenly felt the need to beat his chest like some Neanderthal. My God, he wasn't in a position to do so; he didn't have the right.

He saw her green eyes darken to the color of rich moss, saw her pupils dilate. The scar over her lip turned white.

Then her lashes swept down, concealing her emotions.

And her hand went right up the inside of his thigh, all the way to the top, where she paused a millisecond longer than both of them knew was necessary.

Images flipped through his mind of their one night together, so sharp, so clear, it could have happened just yesterday rather than three months ago.

No sense worrying about an embarrassing arousal. It was a fact now. A hard fact.

"Whitney!" How the devil had he suddenly become a soprano?

She stood, looked him right in the eyes. "Yes?" Innocence dripped from her voice.

"What the hell are you doing?"

"Determining that your inseam is thirty-five and three-quarters. Now, if you're serious about those purple Creepers, I'll need to know so I can adjust the hem accordingly."

"I'm not wearing the damned Creepers, and you were *not* determining my inseam." Upset, out of sorts, he stuck his face right in hers. How could she be so *un*affected! She just stood there looking all cool and sexy and fresh.

She held up the cloth tape measure with her thumbnail still resting on the black hash mark. "See for yourself, Dyl. Thirty-five and three-quarters."

He had the most irrational urge to haul her to him, to kiss that sassy mouth.

She must have read his intent, because she stepped back, turned around and fussed with the stack of stationery on the corner of Karl's mahogany desk.

Dylan took a deep breath.

"Hey, buddy," Jack called. "If you don't need us for a while, Mark and I are gonna head out."

Dylan suspected they were going to plan some kind of bachelor party. He didn't want to think about that right now.

"Fine. I'll see you later at the house." Jack, Patrick and Mark were staying at the Montgomery estate.

Doing a credible imitation of a fast-moving whirlwind, Patrick streaked across the store and smacked right into Dylan's legs, his skinny arms squeezing like a boa constrictor. "'Bye, Dylan."

"'Bye, sport." And like a five-year-old with energy to spare, Patrick changed direction and skipped passed his dad, flicking the coat sleeve on a mannequin and giggling when it wobbled and nearly toppled.

Dylan shook his head, smiled. From the corner of his eye, he saw Karl come out of the dressing room, a light gray sport coat suspended from the hanger in his hand.

"Whoa, Karl. That's my jacket you're about to put on the display floor."

Karl frowned, glanced at the garment in his hand. "Why, you are right. I saw the high quality and automatically assumed it was one of mine."

Dylan grinned. "It *was* one of yours."

"Quite right. I'll just hang it back in the room for you."

Dylan looked back at Whitney. "So, are we done measuring?"

"I don't know. Do you *want* to be?"

"Woman, that sass is going to get you in trouble."

She tsked. "You really should save that kind of banter for your intended, you know."

He narrowed his eyes. Now he realized what her game was. "You're still mad at me."

"Me? Mad? Why would you think that?"

"Because I know you, Slim. And don't you dare deny it."

"You're reading stuff in where it's not. Guilty conscious, Dylan?"

Damn right he had a guilty conscious. He was engaged to one woman and having fantasies about another.

His best friend…who'd also been his lover.

And now that she was actually eye level with him rather than on her knees, he could see that Karl was right. She looked as though she hadn't been sleeping well, wasn't quite up to par.

"You been eating right, Slim?"

She frowned, glanced away. "Sure."

He hooked a finger under her chin, turned her face back to him. "Tell the truth and shame the devil."

She smiled as he'd known she would.

"You know me. Sometimes I forget. I've pulled some late nights sewing."

"We can't have you sacrificing your health. Karl?" He raised his voice, waited until he had the other man's attention. "I'm going to steal your assistant for a bit, make her eat something."

"No—"

"Hush, Whitney. That wasn't a question, it was a statement."

"A very good idea," Karl seconded.

Dylan ran his tongue over his teeth when he saw Whitney bristle. Smart man that he was, he ducked into the dressing room and changed back into his clothes, half expecting her to follow him.

A little disappointed when she didn't.

God, what was with him?

He left the tuxedo on the hanger, knowing that the alterations would be made even on this short notice.

"Ready?" he asked, stopping in front of Whitney.

"Do I have a choice?"

"Of course. Everyone has a choice."

"Then my choice would be not to eat."

"Then *my* choice would be to toss you over my shoulder and take you with me anyway."

"Well, that's a challenge if I ever heard one. Think you're man enough to do it?"

His brows shot up. From any other woman that statement might have sounded like a poke at the ego. With Whitney it was a dare between buddies. At least it would have been before their night together.

For some reason he wanted to pick up the challenge as a man. He had an irrational urge to seduce her into submission. Hell, these caveman scenarios running through his mind were confusing him. And they were going to get him in big trouble.

"Do you want to find out just how manly I am? I

mean, that short skirt's not exactly designed for a scuffle. You could win the match, sure. Then again, you could lose and end up stopping traffic on the road out there. What do you say?''

''I say you're acting really weird and that I better go with you just to make sure you don't wig out and scare the daylights out of some tourist or something.''

He slung his arm across her shoulder. ''That's my buddy.''

She looked at him sharply.

He couldn't hold the look. There was no other way around it. What they'd done together three months ago had changed things between them, put a strain on their relationship, made every look or touch or comment feel as though it were loaded with innuendo.

Or was it just *him* feeling this way?

He steered her through the door and out onto the cobbled courtyard stones. A fountain splashed like rain and wind rustled the leaves of the oak tree.

He opened his mouth, closed it, then annoyed that he felt so wishy-washy, blazed ahead. ''You know I said it before…uh, that what we did could complicate things.''

''And I told you only if we let it.''

''It's hard not to.''

''Dylan, if we'd made more out of it back then, we would have been in a mess now. I mean, look at you. You're engaged to be married! A person who's interested in a relationship doesn't get engaged to someone else three months later.''

''The marriage thing was mainly business. And you said—''

She turned to him, put her fingers over his lips. Her eyes looked pinched, full of emotion, as though she might cry.

His heart took a painful dive.

He'd only made her cry once in his life, when she was fifteen, and he'd sworn never to do it again.

He covered her fingers, kissed the pads, held her gaze. "What is it, Slim?"

Whitney felt as if the lump in her throat was going to burn a hole clear through her neck. The tenderness in his voice, the gentleness in his fingers, was going to undo her. She'd been having more trouble with her emotions lately, felt like a leaky watering pot the majority of the time, and there was no good reason for it—except that her hormones were on the fritz.

And right now she didn't need Dylan to remind her of what she'd said that night. She'd told him that nothing would change, but that was a lie. For her, everything had changed. But she'd wanted to see how it affected Dylan—how it affected him after time had passed. It was a lesson she'd learned about life from her mother.

When she was ten years old she'd found a wounded bird and had nursed it back to health. She'd wanted to keep that sweet little sparrow in a cage, love it, make it hers for life. But Mom had said that wasn't fair. The bird had been free before she'd come into its life, and it should have the chance to fly free again. Then it would have a choice, whether to come back to her or not. *If you love something, set it free. If it returns, then it is meant to be.* The sound of her mother's voice, even now after fifteen years, was so strong.

And Dylan had come back to her. But certainly not as she'd expected.

She wanted to tell him the dilemma she faced—*they* faced, actually. But something held her back. She needed to know for sure just how deeply his feelings ran for Cori.

So she lied, again, even though the words burned like acid on her tongue.

"It's nothing, Dyl. It just feels weird, you getting married and all." She forced a smile, ran her fingers through her hair, mussed it and let it fall in her face to hide her expression. "And you know I get misty at weddings."

He cocked a brow. "We're not at a wedding."

"Well, close enough. I've seen the bride in her dress and the groom in his tuxedo. My imagination can supply the rest of the details. So I'm getting maudlin in advance." Her chin jutted out. "Want to make something of it?"

"No. I want to feed you so you'll get a little more color in those cheeks."

"My cheeks are fine. You're just not used to the new look of skintone blush rather than rosy-hued definition."

"And this new look also calls for dark circles and—"

"Dylan?"

"What?"

"Hush, would you? I've only got dibs on you for six more days before you're another woman's property. Let's not waste it bickering about the color of my face powder or how well my concealer works."

"You'll still have dibs on me, Whit."

Exclusive dibs, she wanted to say, but didn't. "You know what I mean."

It appeared that he didn't want to let the subject go. He shoved his hands into the pockets of his gabardine slacks. He'd left his sport coat back at the tux shop, and the sleeves of his black, button-down shirt were rolled to his elbows. A gold-plated watch circled his wrist. It was the same one she'd given him when he'd graduated from Stanford University. Functional rather than flashy, not cheap, but in no way pricey.

It touched her that he still wore it.

"I'll *never* be a woman's *property.*"

She brought her gaze back to his face, and this time when her smile came, it was genuine, not forced. He looked so petulant, like a little boy defending his right to play with an action figure that somebody had called a doll.

She hooked her arm through his, started them moving again. "How do you feel about ice cream for lunch?"

"I told Karl I was going to tend to your health, not send you on a sugar high."

"I won't tell if you won't."

"Are you kidding? Karl can smell ice cream from fifty paces. He'll know. Besides, I didn't eat breakfast and I'm starving. How about a sandwich first, if I promise ice cream afterward?"

"Well, if you insist. Can't have you wasting away. You need your stamina," she teased.

He shook his head, gave a playful lunge, which she jumped back from with a shriek. Their playfulness brought smiling gazes from the shop owners who stood in their doorways drinking in the spring

air and watching the customers strolling the courtyard.

The antics of Whitney and Dylan could have been
the same as any engaged couple goofing around.

The difference was, he was engaged to somebody
else.

The Courtyard Cottage was a small bistro with casual Mediterranean decor and patio dining where bridal couples could sit among the pots of colorful im-
patiens and geraniums and have a panoramic view of
the specialty boutiques so they could plan their shopping strategy.

Although Whitney and Dylan didn't fall into the
engaged category, they chose to sit outside and soak
up the atmosphere of the open-air courtyard. Birds
sang in the oak tree in the center of the plaza. A
small waterfall splashed and wind chimes tinkled.

Dylan held out Whitney's chair, waited until she
was seated, then sat across from her.

"Want to order some wine?"

She kept her head down, her eyes on the menu.
"None for me, thanks."

Dylan reached over and tipped down her menu.
His brown eyes were intense and probing, his voice
softly curious. "If I didn't know better I'd say you'd
sworn off liquor." He didn't add, *after our night together,* but he might as well have. It was like a silent
shout between them.

She shrugged. "Unlike some people I could name
who appear to have the week off, *I* have to work.
And Uncle Karl frowns on employees falling asleep
over the cash register."

He leaned back in his chair. "Employees, huh.
Aren't you a full partner in that business by now?"

"Yes. But Uncle Karl is still officially the boss."

"So you tell yourself. You could make changes if you wanted."

"I know. But I'm not ready."

"Do I hear a hint of fear?"

"No. I just haven't built up enough of an inventory to branch out with women's designs in the shop. I will soon, though."

Kevin Gardner, master chef and owner of the bistro, stopped at their table. "Well, look who the cat's dragged in. I get to see Whitney often enough, but it's a treat to see you both here together."

Such an innocent statement. There was no call for the way Whitney's adrenaline rushed—as though she were doing something sneaky and wrong; as though her transgressions and emotions were written right across her face; as though Kevin had picked up on the fact that she was in love with Dylan Montgomery and that it was too late because he was planning to get married in a week's time to someone else.

Dylan stood and shook hands with Kevin. "How's it going?"

"Can't complain. Plenty of folks gearing up for June weddings. Aside from bridal clientele, I'm doing a brisk business. Do you two know what you want?"

Whitney didn't want a thing. That last head rush had made her stomach quake again. But she didn't want to answer forty questions—from either of these guys. If she didn't eat, not only would Dylan prod, Kevin would be stopping by to inform Uncle Karl that all was not well with his niece.

Small communities could be both a blessing and a bane.

She ordered a house salad and iced tea.

She should have known that both men would look at her as if she'd insulted the pope. Kevin paused, refusing to write. Dylan opened his mouth to admonish—Whitney knew him well. She cut him off.

"Sorry, Kevin, but I've got my heart set on ice cream and I'm not going to eat so much that I can't enjoy it."

Kevin's ruddy face was the picture of affront. "You know I don't serve ice cream. Shame on you, flaunting the fact that you are intending to visit my competition."

She laughed. "Hardly competition. And Dylan said he was starving. He'll order enough for the both of us."

He did, and Kevin went back to his mesquite grill a happy man once more.

"You're not usually such a cheap date, Slim."

She winked. "Be thankful for small favors. Tomorrow I might have a yen for lobster."

"Then you'd be paying."

"Now, who's talking cheap?"

Something in their bantering had touched a chord in him. She could see it in the way his forehead pleated. Dylan always got three creases across his brow when he was upset or worried or baffled. She ruled out baffled, toyed with upset, and settled on worried.

Reaching across the table, she nudged his baby finger, slipped her own around it in their special pact. It was their sign to come clean with whatever was on their mind.

He looked down at their linked fingers, and a small dimple winked in his cheek. His brown eyes were filled with something that looked an awful lot like love.

Whitney stopped herself from going down that path.

"Give it up, buddy."

"You always read me."

"Like a book. What's up?"

"Business."

"Bad?"

"Worse than bad." He sighed, pinched the bridge of his nose. "I could lose it, Whitney."

"No." The word was barely a whisper. Her breath suspended in disbelief and despair. Montgomery Industries was Dylan's life.

He nodded.

"What happened?"

"Dad."

She groaned, not really needing to hear anything past that single word. She gave his finger a squeeze, urged him on anyway. "What did he do?"

"Gambled the company funds on a risky venture."

"And you didn't know?"

"No. He didn't go through the accountant. He did it personally, used both the business and the house as collateral. He financed a guy who claimed to have patented a special stabilizer chip for cruise ships. It didn't pan out and the company folded before it got off the ground. Since Dad was the silent owner, the bank is demanding repayment of the loan or they'll invoke the liens on the business and the estate. I don't have near that amount in liquid assets."

"And you just found out about this recently?"

"In February." Right after he'd left her the last

time. "I knew we had a loan with the bank that we were making payments on. I didn't know Dad had upped the loan, signed away most of our stock, agreed to a balloon payment."

"He must have had a certain amount of confidence in the venture."

"What my father had was a certain amount of *arrogance* that kept him from thinking about who and what he was putting on the line on a whim. He never said a word, but I know what he'd planned—to brag when he made a pile of money, to wave it in our faces and make sure we all knew who was king. And it's just like him to die and leave the mess for me to clean up."

"Oh, Dylan, what are you going to do?" She rarely heard him sound this bitter. Dylan was the kind of guy who laughed on the outside, keeping his pain and dissatisfaction well hidden.

"I've already done it." He looked at her, and there was actual apology in his eyes. "I'm getting married."

"Huh?" She was certain she had a look on her face that was as dumb as her single word. She knew he was getting married, but because of a debt?

"William Spencer approached me several months back about a merger. I didn't like his terms and I turned him down. That was before I knew about the loan on the defunct company. When I realized how bad things were, what could, and *would* happen to all our assets, I rethought the deal."

"Which was?" She was getting a bad feeling here.

"A merger and financial backing in exchange for marriage to Spencer's daughter."

"Cori?"

"Yes."

"That's archaic!" Her outburst startled a sparrow who'd been picking at a crumb of bread by their table. In a frantic beat of wings, it took off, emitting a flurry of indignant cheeps. She flinched, feeling the bird's wings beat the air right by her head. *An arranged marriage. For money. Impossible.*

"I know. It's just another thing dear old Dad set in motion before he died, another area he meddled in. He's the one who put a bug in Spencer's ear about marriage. Then he put Spencer right in my path, knowing I probably couldn't resist a plum opportunity involving lasers."

Her head spun trying to understand what he was saying, what it might mean for her—for their baby.

"Okay, that explains your motivation, but what about Cori? Why in the world would she agree to marry *you?*"

Although this wasn't a laughing matter, she nearly did so when his hairline shifted in surprise. He was obviously trying to figure out whether or not he'd been insulted.

"I didn't mean it like that, Dylan. There's a list as long as my arm of women who'd agree that you're definitely a catch. I'm asking why Cori Spencer would agree to a modern day marriage of convenience."

"As long as your arm, huh?"

"Put your ego away and don't evade."

"You're tough, Whit. I asked her the same thing— what she was getting out of the bargain. She said she had her reasons." He shrugged. "She wasn't willing to share them just then, and I didn't push."

Whitney nodded. She didn't need to pry to know

Cori's reasons. A strong woman, a detective, Cori wouldn't want to admit she was head over heels in love with a man who'd only asked for her hand in marriage to save his company.

And aside from what was at stake for Dylan's employees, and his family, Whitney truly liked Cori Spencer. She knew what it was like to feel that deep-flowing current of love for a man.

For Dylan.

A crummy part of her wanted to ignore the other woman's feelings, wanted to jut out her chin and say, "He was *mine* first. Tough luck."

But he wasn't hers. Not really. And not in that way.

Now more than ever she realized it would be best to keep silent about her own news—at least until after the wedding.

She wouldn't be the cause of putting Dylan's company in jeopardy.

With her stomach roiling like a caldron of acid, she merely picked at her salad. As soon as Dylan laid down his fork, she grabbed his wrist, checked the dial of his watch.

"Oh, look at the time. I should get back to the shop. Uncle Karl's got an outside appointment this afternoon."

"What about that ice cream?"

She stood, waved at Kevin, who came right over with the check. He was used to her being in a hurry. "Guess I'll have to take a rain check. We'll just add a vanilla-dipped cone to the list of foot massages you owe me."

Dylan pulled several bills out of his wallet, handed them to Kevin without even looking at the total, then placed his hand at the small of Whitney's back, steering her through the foliage and out into the courtyard, his soft chuckle stirring the hair at her temple.

"That's going to get pretty messy if you collect both at once."

"I don't know about that. Sounds pretty good to me."

"Uh-uh. I know you, Slim. You go into a trance when somebody rubs your feet. That cone's guaranteed to melt right down the front of you."

She really didn't want to talk about melting and fronts and rubbing. She was feeling the strain of trying to be jovial and friendly. Of pretending.

The sooner this day ended, the better off she'd be.

When they got back to Delaney's, Whitney went right for the dressing room, retrieved Dylan's pale charcoal sport coat, and handed it to him.

"Thanks for lunch, Dylan. I'll see you before the wedding, I'm sure." She smiled, pushed her hair behind her ears.

"Well, I hope so. I'd thought we could head over to Monterey, maybe dig through some of those shops you love so, gorge ourselves on fish and chowder."

Whitney could already feel the salad she'd had for lunch rising up to rebel. It would tear her up to spend time with Dylan, knowing she had to keep quiet, knowing he'd pledged himself to another woman. Even though saving his company was his primary concern, he had to have some sort of special feelings for Cori Spencer.

Karl came out from the dressing room, his lips pursed beneath his gray mustache as he glanced from Whitney to Dylan. Out of habit, he took the jacket from Dylan, held it as he slipped his arms through the sleeves. Karl brushed his hand over the shoulder seams, smoothed, fussed.

Dylan shifted from foot to foot. For some reason it seemed as though both Whitney and Karl were anxious for him to leave.

Or was it just his own self-consciousness? He shouldn't be looking for excuses to stay. Besides, he needed to get back to the estate, check in with his mother. With his rushed, last-minute arrival in town, the engagement party and the tux fitting, he hadn't had a chance to catch up with his family.

"Okay, I'll head out so you can get back to work. I'll call you."

"Sure."

Unable to think of another reason to stall, he shook hands with Karl, brushed a finger down Whitney's pale cheek, then let himself out the door and walked the two blocks to where his car was parked.

It's a wonder he didn't run over somebody as he negotiated the narrow streets of town, because his mind definitely wasn't on his driving.

It was on Whitney.

And that wild measuring experience she'd put him through.

And the way she'd looked in that sexy little miniskirt and skin-cleaving top.

He somehow made it onto the winding coastal highway. Even over the rush of sea air skimming the convertible, he was listening to the engine, alert for noises that would indicate trouble. His gaze recorded road conditions, gauged the distance between cars, the pitch of the road, the bank of a curve that would indicate the safest speed to hit it. Once determined, of course, he would push it just over its limit. A game for sure, but he was always in control.

Of the car, at least.

He didn't feel in control where Whitney was concerned, though. She'd sent him off three months ago, made him believe her flippant words.

Hell, maybe he'd *needed* to believe them—that there really couldn't be more between them, that they would always be just friends.

So he'd held on to that assurance, accepted Spencer's offer with hardly a twinge for what it would mean to his and Whitney's relationship. Actually, he'd been so distraught over the imminent downfall of the company, he hadn't thought of anything but that.

He'd been in San Francisco. Whitney had been here. Out of sight, out of mind. Sort of.

Now that he'd seen her again, though, touched her, remembered…he wondered how he could have made such a commitment to another woman—regardless of the state of his company.

Surely there was another way to get around this problem. He'd chosen the most expedient. But why? For crying out loud, he was a confirmed bachelor. What had possessed him to agree to marriage?

Losing the Montgomery estate, he answered himself. Losing the business and its income that kept his mom and sister with a roof over their heads and money in their accounts. He was responsible for his family, had picked up the mantle of his father, sworn to take care of them.

Just as he'd always taken care of them.

When Randolph had turned the brunt of his temper and foul disposition on Mom or Candice, Dylan had stepped into the breach, been their buffer, protected, taken the heat. From a very young age he'd fallen into a habit of taking care of the women in his life.

And if he let the business die, he'd be letting his family down, too. He couldn't allow that to happen.

He reached into his coat pocket for his appointment book to look up Mark Forrester's cell phone number. Although business was pretty much on hold for the week—until after the wedding—it wouldn't hurt to get a jump on the preliminaries. They'd need to set up an appointment with attorneys, the accountants, the shareholders. Good thing he and Cori weren't planning a honeymoon. There would be a lot to do after the wedding took place.

A piece of ivory-embossed stationery fell out as he opened his daily planner wallet.

Frowning, trying to keep one eye on the road, he grabbed for the paper, unfolded it, quickly scanned the six words written in boldly flowing cursive...

And nearly ran the Porsche right over the cliff.

You're going to be a daddy.

Chapter Six

Dylan jerked the wheel and overcorrected. The back end of the sports car—going too fast in the first place—fishtailed and nearly came around on him. Quick reflexes had him gaining control, slowing, pulling over to the side of the road.

He needed a minute to collect himself.

Dust swirled around the car from the sudden stop on the shoulder, settling over the buff interior in a gritty film.

Sweat beaded at his temples as his heart pumped and his mind flitted from one thought to the next, so disjointed he was making himself dizzy.

Regardless of the fact that he was a newly engaged man, there was only one woman he'd made love with in the past year.

Whitney Emerson.

His best friend.

Karl Delaney's niece.

And this was Karl Delaney's stationery, the man's trademark. So, okay, it wasn't advice, it was information. A deviation from the norm. But there was still no mistaking the paper, the M.O. that might as well have had Karl's fingerprints stamped all over it.

Further damning were Dylan's own memories—which were so vivid right now he was growing uncomfortable. They hadn't been careful. Hell, he'd never dreamed at the beginning of that night that there would be a need for protection. He didn't normally carry condoms with him to business meetings.

And that's where he'd been coming from that day.

Besides, he distinctly remembered fighting that odd and blinding attraction to Whitney, remembered that he'd promised himself he could certainly exercise a little more control.

Well, just look how good that control had turned out, what it had gotten him. His best friend pregnant.

And him not finding out until he was already engaged to another woman.

Why hadn't she told him?

Raking a hand through his hair, he tucked the note into his pocket, checked the side and rearview mirrors, then stabbed the accelerator, putting the Porsche into a gravel-spitting, rubber-burning U-turn.

Whitney Emerson had some explaining to do. No wonder she was pale as a ghost. "Skintone blush, my butt."

THROUGH THE ARCHED windows that looked out onto the street, Karl saw the red Porsche circle the block. He smiled to himself and slipped into the back room where he'd be out of sight, but still able to see and hear and monitor how well his latest endeavor had worked.

It pleased him to offer advice—or to give a gentle nudge when need be. And he'd certainly been happy to do so regarding the Spencer wedding. Now, *that* was a mess if ever there was one. The players were all wrong—or at least, terribly mixed up. Any fool could see this. So why in the world had it gone this far?

But since it had, Karl considered it his duty and his pleasure to set it right.

He gave a tug to his cuffs, stroked his mustache, and angled the back room door just a little wider. Not wide enough to be detected, but enough so that he could see and hear.

Dylan burst through the street-side door with a speed that startled Whitney. Karl saw her pale; he felt a little bad that he hadn't prepared her. Then again, catching her off guard might be just the thing to get matters back in line. The girl kept too much inside, tried to carry too much on her shoulders— alone. When he'd stopped by her home a week ago, he'd seen the box to determine pregnancy in the wastebasket of her bathroom. He'd waited for her to confide in him. She hadn't. He'd waited for her to call Dylan. She hadn't.

It didn't occur to him that the results might have been negative. There was a test box, so there was a baby growing.

And he was certain Dylan was the father.

Whitney had been in love with the boy since she was but a child. Oh, she'd had other beaus, but those relationships had not grown serious, had not lasted.

Funny how these two kids had kept so busy they hadn't stopped long enough to recognize the true depth of their feelings for one another.

But Karl had known. He'd seen the look on Whitney's face when Dylan came into town back in January, the same delight she'd always shown—the love.

And he'd seen the devastation when they'd entered Cori Spencer's engagement party and learned that Dylan Montgomery was the groom.

Karl still didn't know how that information had not reached him. He was usually the first to know gossip or plans or happenings within the community. And even though Gracie had only known about the upcoming wedding for a mere two days before the party, it still dented his heart that she had not confided in him.

He smoothed his mustache, took a breath. He did not want to think about Grace Montgomery and dented hearts. Right now, his niece's heart was the one torn and in need of healing.

Cocking his head, he listened carefully.

"Dylan?"

"I'm going to be a daddy?"

Karl pursed his lips. He'd expected a little more finesse. But the direct route would do—even though it did have a bit of an accusatory tone to it.

"You are?"

Caught up in Dylan's words, Whitney's comeback made Karl frown. He straightened and nearly gave away his hiding place as he knocked over a stack of shirts. Luckily he caught them before disaster happened.

"According to Karl's note, I am."

"Karl's note?"

There appeared to be an echo in the room. Why was his niece repeating everything the boy said?

For a bare instant Karl had reservations about his meddling. Surely he hadn't misjudged the significance of that drugstore box.

"Do you recognize the stationery?"

"Yes."

"Why didn't you tell me?"

"Why in the world would you think that note applies to me?"

"Because it was in my pocket, and I was your first lover!"

Oh! Karl felt himself grow a little warm. He hadn't expected to be privy to quite *this* much intimate information. And he felt an extra twinge of guilt because he was skulking in the back when it was delivered.

But he was not worried enough to show himself. Not yet, anyway. In fact, it pleased him to know this private information, that Dylan was the first man for Whitney; it made him feel like a proud papa—or uncle, rather.

Once she'd reached the age of twenty-one, he'd not felt so harried and concerned over Whitney's love life. Knowing now that she'd waited for Dylan all these years, until she was twenty-seven, was a good thing.

His sister, Katia, would have been proud, would have hugged him and told him he'd done a fine job raising her daughter. His eyes misted as he got caught up in the past.

Then Whitney laughed, bringing Karl's attention back to the matter at hand. He knew the sound was fake, brittle. At any other time, he figured Dylan would have realized that, too. But Dylan could be excused because he was obviously distraught.

"Dylan, we've been over this before." She pushed the note back across the counter as though it were a venomous snake. "You're making too much out of the experience."

Karl saw Dylan go red in the face. Well, he didn't blame him. That was a blow to the ego—albeit an inadvertent one, he allowed. Nobody was thinking straight here.

But he'd pushed enough for now, he had to let the kids play it out. At least this time. And there was still hope.

"Are you saying you're not pregnant?"

"I'm saying Uncle Karl probably put that note in the wrong pocket."

"Oh."

Nyet! Do not believe her! Look in her eyes, Dylan—you know her better!

"Remember when Uncle Karl came out of the dressing room with your coat? He didn't know it was yours. That's probably when the mix-up occurred."

"But no one else was in the shop."

"Da," Karl whispered. Yes. "You are a smart boy." He glanced at Whitney. *Tell him, my dove.*

"We've always got jackets here in need of tailoring. Don't give it another thought, Dylan. You're getting married in less that a week. Concentrate on that." She came out from behind the counter, turned him and gave him a friendly nudge toward the door. "Now, scoot before you give me any more near heart attacks."

Karl saw Dylan hesitate and gaze into Whitney's eyes. *Da.* Yes. *Look hard.*

Then, of all things, Dylan nodded, turned and went through the door! Karl leaped forward, nearly shouted in frustration. But it was too late. For today, at least.

"Uncle Karl?" Whitney said, her voice raised. "You can come out of hiding now."

Karl sniffed, tugged at his cuffs again, squared his shoulders and stepped through the doorway of the dressing area, remembering at the last second to grab a stack of jewel-colored shirts as though he'd merely been doing inventory.

"Are you speaking to me?"

Whitney couldn't even find the energy to laugh at her uncle's poor attempt at subterfuge. She was holding on to her emotions by a mere thread and she was terribly afraid that any second now she was going to snap in two.

While Karl separated a handful of mango and melon shirts and stacked them atop a pile that was already on the verge of teetering, she looked away, took a breath and tried to gather her emotions before they spilled out in a river of shame and grief.

Across the courtyard at Leena's bridal shop, a young girl posed in her wedding dress, beaming as her mother and Leena looked on. Then the mother stepped forward, her face lined with pride and love, and draped a strand of pearls around her daughter's neck, linking one generation to the next with a mere clasp.

Tears came out of nowhere, stung Whitney's eyes and throat, tears of envy, of emotions she couldn't quite name. Oh, God, she missed her mother.

She didn't realize the tears had spilled over until Karl audibly sucked in a breath, touched her cheek, pulled her right against his chest and held her as any father would have done, comforted, soothed, apologized as though wishing he could take the sadness and hurt on his own shoulders, spare her.

She tried to pull back. "I'll ruin your beautiful suit."

"Never mind the suit. Why did you not tell him, my dove?"

"How did you know?" she whispered instead of answering.

"I saw the test box."

"Oh."

"Why didn't you tell Dylan?"

"Because he's getting married."

"But he would not be if you told him about the baby."

Whitney straightened and stepped back a pace. Karl fussed, patted, but let her go. "Uncle Karl, you shouldn't have given him that note."

"And you should have told him of the baby so it would not have been necessary."

"I can't."

"Why?"

"Because then he *would* call off the wedding."

Karl threw up his hands, scowled. "Exactly my point! So what is the problem? Do you *want* him to marry Cori Spencer? Granted she is a lovely girl, but she is not the woman for him."

Whitney rubbed her right eye. A dull ache lurked behind the socket, deep in her skull, warning of a migraine. She willed the pain away.

"There's more to it than that."

"What, I ask you?"

Whitney shook her head, cursed the tears that welled and spilled over again. For the life of her she couldn't seem to control her emotions. This had never happened to her before, and she didn't like it, didn't like feeling so close to the edge, as if she was about to slip over, to shatter into a thousand tiny pieces and never be whole again.

She had to keep it together. She needed time, space. With a little practice, some time to get past this ache, to accept, to plan, she'd be fine.

But right now, she was not fine. Right now her cheeks were wet and her hands were shaking and her insides quivered and her throat ached. One false move and she would very likely start screaming. And if she started screaming, she just might never stop.

On top of that, Karl was looking at her with compassion, with the kind of look a parent gives when they feel helpless to make it better.

Oh, he'd tried—with his note in Dylan's pocket. But that wouldn't fix it. That wouldn't get Dylan his merger, his money to pay the bad debt his father had created, the means to insure the solvency and safety of his company and his mother and sister's home, their life-style. All the things she knew Dylan accepted as his responsibilities. Obligations he'd shouldered since he was a teenager.

No, Uncle Karl had meant well, but it was the wrong avenue to take. She wasn't absolutely certain which was the right one, but she did know she had to make it through this next week, make it until Dylan got married. Then she'd reassess.

She didn't have any intention of keeping their child a secret forever; Dylan deserved to know about his baby.

Just not yet.

Not until his company was safe. His family's home was safe. His peace of mind was safe.

Then they'd deal with her dilemma.

"Uncle Karl, I need some time away."

"Ah, Whitney, my dove—"

She held up her hand. "Please," she whispered,

wanting nothing more than to ease back into her uncle's arms. But to do that would only release another wave of painful emotions. She had to get a grip. "I can't tell Dylan about the baby right now, and you've got to promise me that you won't, either."

"But—"

"Promise me, Uncle Karl." She bit her bottom lip, knuckled away her wimpy tears. "I need for you to keep the baby a secret. For now."

Karl sighed. "I do not understand this, but I will promise."

"Thank you." She hugged him hard, inhaled the familiar, comforting scent of Old Spice cologne, felt a pang of nostalgia so strong her knees nearly buckled.

That spicy scent was what she remembered about that fateful day fifteen years ago. She'd been staying the weekend at the Montgomerys, having a sleepover with Dylan's sister Candice, while her mother and dad and sister, Jeanice, had flown into Las Vegas for a gymnastic meet Jeanice was competing in. Whitney hadn't been able to go because she'd broken her leg in a horseback riding accident just days before and hadn't yet mastered the crutches. Knowing she'd only slow the family down—especially in a city as crowded and bustling as Las Vegas—she'd opted to stay with Candice.

She'd been twelve; Candice was thirteen.

And over the smell of nail polish had come the unmistakable scent of Old Spice.

Whitney had been ecstatic. She loved it when Uncle Karl visited, which wasn't often. More times than not, the family went to San Francisco. Mother had said there were reasons that made it difficult for Uncle Karl to come to Montgomery Beach, that it made him sad.

And that day he had indeed looked sad. But a different kind of sad. She'd known in an instant something dreadful was wrong. Her mouth had opened on a silent scream, and Uncle Karl had simply held out his arms, scooped her to his chest, enveloped her in the comforting, familiar scent of Old Spice, promised her everything would be all right, that in time it wouldn't hurt so bad, but no matter what, she would always have him and he would take care, make it right.

He'd moved here to Montgomery Beach. And she'd seen that sadness her mother had talked about, a sadness that was different than for the death of his sister and brother-in-law and niece.

Whitney had wondered if he'd left someone behind in San Francisco, but he'd never said, had always sidestepped when she'd tried to broach the subject.

She'd always felt as if he'd made a great sacrifice because of her—even though she wasn't absolutely certain what it was he'd given up, or the magnitude of what he'd let go. Oh, he denied it, but the feeling was still there. He'd relocated for her, left his life in San Francisco, and come here.

He'd never married.

She was his only family. She wondered if he wanted or needed more, had an idea he did.

And because she'd been the cause of Uncle Karl's sacrifice, she couldn't do the same to Dylan.

She wouldn't be the cause of his hidden sadness, the ruination of his life-style, his livelihood, wouldn't stand in the way of the possibility that Cori Spencer

just might turn out to be the great love of his life—
that Cori's hidden love for him would blossom and
be returned.

And though that thought nearly tore her heart in
two, she didn't want to win him by default, to trap
him, to cause his life to be *less* than it could have
been.

So she was the one who'd be doing the sacrificing
this time.

And she just had to make it through the coming
week.

She gave Uncle Karl another tight hug that con-
veyed apology and appreciation and love.

"Can I stay at the beach house for a while?"

"Of course. You know you are welcome to use it
anytime. But are you certain you want to run away
like this?"

She winced. She wasn't the sort to run away. Usually.

"I just need time."

He nodded. "Then take it. You know where the
key is."

Before she could escape, the phone rang. Uncle
Karl answered, then gave her a look of apology as
he punched the Hold button. "I'm sorry, my dove.
It is Leena from the bridal shop and she can see
through the window that you are still here." He held
out the receiver to her.

Oh, no, Whitney thought. She knew what Leena
wanted. The dress alterations. She'd completely forgotten—and no wonder. Her finger hovered over the
hold button. Her palms were damp and her stomach
churned. Finally she pressed the red flashing square.

"Leena," she greeted carefully, composing her thoughts—her evasions.

"Hi, doll. I'm just being my usual neurotic self. You will have the Spencer gown finished by Friday, won't you? I've arranged one final fitting…"

"Uh, Leena, I'm not sure—"

A swiftly indrawn breath, a near shriek. "Do not do this to me, doll. You know I have a weak heart. The gown is so extravagant. Just think of the money—my reputation. I promised, knowing you were good for the alterations. No one comes through quicker and more consistently than you do. You must!"

Whitney could barely get a word in edgewise. Leena was always so dramatic, spoke so quickly, hardly pausing to take a breath.

But could she do it? She'd never reneged on a deal. This was different, though.

This was a dress for Dylan's bride.

The man Whitney loved.

God, she'd agreed to do the dress really fast—but that was *before* she'd known who all the interested parties were.

She put a hand over her heart, rubbed, didn't even realize what she was doing, didn't even realize that her chest hurt, *physically* hurt.

"Whitney? Doll, are you still there? You know I will pay you extra. The Spencers will pay you extra. My gracious, the groom's family is worth a mint! Please—"

"Leena," Whitney said, the very softness of her voice breaking into Leena's tirade. It was as though something silent had reached through the telephone wires and stopped the other woman cold, had opened her eyes and her heart and shown her something was amiss, that there was hurt. "I'll have the dress ready." The words were difficult to get past the horrible lump in her throat.

"Oh, my, are you all right?"

"Fine."

"I can probably get someone—"

"There's no one else on this short notice, Leena. I said I'd do it and I will. It's just that I'm going out of town for a few days. I'll take it with me, though."

"Are you certain?"

"Yes." *No, I'm not certain. My heart's breaking and I'm trying desperately to hold it together.* "I'll have it back to you by Friday."

AN UNSETTLING FEELING nagged at Dylan as he made his way to his family's estate. He couldn't remember ever feeling so on edge in his life.

By rote, he turned off the highway and onto the long winding drive that climbed even higher than the cliff road. Built on a hill overlooking the sea, his family's estate could be seen for miles. The locals likened it to the Hearst Castle of Montgomery Beach and out-of-towners wondered if there would ever come a day when it would be opened to tours.

Dylan's stomach twisted into a tighter knot. If he made the slightest misstep right now, that decision would likely be left up to the bank rather than his family.

The grounds were kept to perfection by an army of gardeners; a service made sure the pool sparkled like an expensive diamond. The water bill alone to keep the lawn green probably supported the city of Montgomery Beach.

The magnificent Mediterranean villa overlooked the Pacific Ocean, and had been standing proud since 1906. Iron balconies decorated each of the many windows and sported the Montgomery coat of arms, passed down from their ancestors in Great Britain.

Five hundred yards from the electronic gate, Dylan pressed the automatic opener on his visor and, timing the opening of the gates, gauged his speed so he could squeak right through before they were all the way open. It was a game he'd perfected as a teen, one that had initially cost him a few new front quarter panels.

The grand circular drive deposited him right by the front door, where he parked behind his sister's black BMW and Mark Forrester's white, 1963 classic Corvette. Jack's Suburban wasn't there, so no telling where his best man and godson were.

Candice's car being in front of the main house instead of at the guest cottage she called home must mean she was spending more time at the main house with Mom now that their father was gone.

Dylan shut off the Porsche's engine, reluctant to go in just yet. He looked at the white stucco structure with its Spanish tile roof. There were happy memories here at this house because of his mom. But he had never felt any real attachment for the monstrous estate. Neither had Candice, which was why she'd moved into the guest cottage set farther back on the grounds. She'd still been somewhat under Daddy's thumb, but with at least a yard's length buffer between them. And when Randolph settled in with his nightly cocktail, it wasn't likely he'd make the trek to the guest cottage to pick on Candy.

But things were different now. Candy didn't have

to duck her father's inflexible principles, didn't have to go along with what he wanted for her life.

So, Dylan was a little surprised that she was still in Montgomery Beach. Probably because of Mom. And to be fair, she did have a circle of friends here—including Whitney.

Feeling his edginess go up a notch, he got out of the car, climbed the concrete steps to the massive front door and let himself in. The marble floors in the grand foyer gave way to rich, gleaming pine in the front living room where floral area rugs added rich decor as well as protection from scuffs. Curving archways and thick plaster walls accented soaring cathedral ceilings with heavy exposed beams reminiscent of the casas of old. There were seven bedroom suites, ten fireplaces, fifteen bathrooms and a kitchen any gourmet would covet. The place was a graceful blend of old and new, hinting of an aristocratic past, yet very much of the moment.

From the parlor came the sound of classical piano music.

Grace Montgomery always played the piano as a way to de-stress.

Dylan moved just inside the room, watched as his beautiful mother poured her heart and soul into the ivory keys of the grand piano. He hadn't seen her play with this much passion and angst since before his father had died. Then again, he hadn't been home much to know of his mother's daily habits.

At fifty-nine, Grace Montgomery was still a beautiful woman. Small and trim, delicate, yet regal. Very correct. Family was everything to her—mainly her children. He couldn't remember a time when he'd ever heard her complain about anything.

Instead she played the piano, the notes taking on a crashing passion that spoke as though in anguished words.

"She's been doing that a lot since you came back to town engaged."

Dylan turned, held out his arm and waited as his sister eased up against his side. They stood like that, arm in arm, for several minutes, just watching their mother play, lost in her own thoughts, her own private world, working through whatever demons chased her. Each knew that when she'd gotten it out of her system, the room would grow silent. That could take minutes or hours.

"What's on her mind?" he asked his sister, keeping his voice low so as not to alert his mother to her audience.

"Beats me."

He gestured with his head that they should leave, and Candice nodded, following him out of the room, past the wide circular staircase and into the kitchen. Surprisingly, the cook wasn't here and they had the room to themselves.

Opening the fridge, he took out a beer. "Want one?"

"Sure."

He twisted the caps, handed a bottle to his sister and clinked the glass necks in silent toast.

"I saw Mark's car out front and figured he'd be with you." The words were more of a question than an observation. Candice could hold her cards pretty close to her chest when she wanted to. Evidently now wasn't much different.

She shrugged. "He took that cell phone of his and headed out toward the pool. Next thing I knew he'd disappeared. I have no idea where. Maybe he's in his room.''

"Waiting for you?"

She gave him her haughtiest look. "No. He is not waiting for me."

"Sure about that, sis?"

She looked away. "He'll get over it."

"Ah, not interested, huh?"

"He's a nice guy."

"But not for you?"

"I don't know. Maybe. Maybe not. I'm restless, Dylan."

"Join the club."

Her blond brows rose and her full rosy lips curved. People were always telling him his sister was a dead ringer for Melanie Griffith, and at that moment, he understood and saw the resemblance.

"You've got no business being part of the restless club seeing as how you're getting married next weekend, brother, dear.''

Very true. Then again, that wasn't the real or the only cause of his restlessness. But he couldn't bring himself to tell Candice about their father's screwup—the sour deal that could well affect the quality of life as she knew it. If the estate was lost, Candy's home went with it. He didn't want to worry her needlessly. He was taking care of things.

Just as he always did.

"Have you talked to Whitney lately?"

Candice frowned. Well, no wonder. She'd mentioned his wedding day and he'd come back with Whitney's name. A slip if there ever was one.

"No, I haven't seen her much. What's up?"

In this, Dylan could confide in his sister. She

wouldn't judge him. She would help clarify his thinking.

He debated for a second, then reached into his pocket, withdrew the piece of ivory stationery, and pushed it across the pine table.

Candice picked it up, her china-blue eyes going wide. "This is Karl Delaney's trademark. Where did you get it?"

"In my jacket pocket."

"In your... My God, Dylan, who did you get pregnant?"

He stood, paced, took a healthy swig of beer, looked down at the dark green bottle. He and Whitney had put away a few beers that night three months ago. He hadn't been drunk, but they'd both been more relaxed, less inhibited than they normally would have been. Their guards had been down. So did that mean their true feelings were exposed? That they'd acted on emotions that had always been there?

What a mess.

"I think Whitney's pregnant."

"You *think?*"

"She says she's not."

Candice got up, moved across the room and took away his beer. "You've obviously had enough. You're not making a bit of sense. This note says *you're* going to be a daddy. You say you *think* Whitney's pregnant. I didn't even know the two of you were involved!"

"We're not." He didn't really have a taste for the beer, so he didn't object to her taking it from him. "I mean, we were for one night, but..." He raked a hand through his hair. "I'm so confused. I don't know what the hell we are."

"Okay, okay." She set the bottles on the counter, pulled him back over to the table, and urged him to sit. "Start at the beginning."

"Well, the beginning starts when we were kids—"

"I know that much. Skip to the baby part."

"Last January, I stopped in town—"

"And you didn't come home?"

"Do you want to hear this or not?"

"I'm not sure, but go ahead."

He sighed. "I stopped in and saw Whitney. We went to Hank's, played some pool, drank more than we should have—not that I'm using that as an excuse, you understand."

"Of course."

"Anyway, one thing led to another. I don't know why it was so different that time. I've always loved Whitney. But I didn't think it was like that."

"So, you made love with her, then left and got engaged to somebody else? I know you're a Casanova, but that's just not like you, Dylan."

"It's a really long story. Whitney convinced me that we'd just gotten carried away with the moment, that we were really just great friends. She didn't want to go for a deeper relationship because she was afraid something would go wrong and we'd lose what we'd come to count on. The closeness of friendship. Plus, she said she was going places career-wise, and didn't want the added stress of trying to make a man-woman thing fly."

Candice raised a brow but kept silent.

"So, I went ahead and left—at her insistence," he added, lest his sister continue to look at him as though he were a typical, low-life *guy.* "And I didn't think about...well, I didn't realize how I'd feel once I saw her again. And now this." He touched a finger to the note. "She say's it's a mistake, but I'm not so sure."

"You know, you can be such a dolt sometimes."

"Thanks a lot."

"Really, Dylan, I love you to death, but have you ever known Karl to make a mistake?"

Her tone held a deep fondness for the Russian tux shop owner. Just as Dylan had, Candice had also secretly coveted Whitney's special relationship with her uncle, wishing at times that they were part of the Delaney clan rather than a Montgomery.

"No...and I *told* him that was my coat he had over his arm."

"You've lost me there, but it doesn't matter. I know Whitney. And so do you. She'd saw off her arm before she'd hurt somebody else. You're engaged to be married in less than a week. She's not going to wreck that for you—or for Cori."

"So you think she's lying?"

Candice shrugged, repositioned the Waterford fruit bowl in the center of the table. "I hate to use such a harsh word. I think she might be doing what she thinks is best for you."

"So what should I do?"

"What do you want to do?"

"Go after her. Find out the truth."

"And then what?"

"I don't know." *Call off the wedding.*

She patted his cheek. "You'll do the right thing. Better get going. Sounds like Mom's winding down on the piano. If she sees you here, you'll never make it out the door. And that possible baby that Whitney might or might not have cooking could likely end up as a teenager before you ever get to the bottom of things.''

Dylan grinned and tugged at his sister's blond locks. ''You've got such an imagination, you ought to go into fiction writing.''

''Maybe I will.''

He realized he'd been focusing solely on himself, and his sister's tone sounded a little off. ''You okay, sis?''

''Just dandy. Now get out of here before Mark finds you. Between him and mother you'll be an old man before you ever make it to the door.''

''Thanks, Candy-Cane.'' He grinned and ducked as a kiwi sailed across the kitchen, aimed at his head. It landed with a splat on the doorjamb. His sister always pretended she hated it when he called her by that nickname. Secretly, he knew she loved it.

He glanced over his shoulder, laughed, then ducked through the door before any more fruit could decorate the walls.

Chapter Seven

For the third time that day, Dylan circled the block in front of Delaney's Tux Shop. He knew his car was visible through the arched windows that faced the street, and hoped Whitney was on the courtyard side of the store. He'd just as soon have a little surprise on his side when he went back to confront her.

The pieces of the puzzle didn't fit—and it was a damn shame it took his sister to point that out. Did he have to be hit over the head with a two-by-four?

His heart felt as though it was sitting in his throat, beating too hard. How many more shocks could his system stand? he wondered. Was it possible for a guy of thirty-two to have a stroke?

He gave up on a close parking spot, wedged the Porsche into a curbside space, and jogged the block to the tux shop.

Karl Delaney looked up, his blue eyes warm with welcome—and relief? He stroked his gray mustache as he came out from behind the counter.

"Dylan, my boy. Back so soon?"

He glanced around the shop. "Where is she?"

Karl shook his head. "Not here."

"Did she already go home?"

"Nyet."

"No? Then do you know where she is?"

"Da."

Dylan waited. "Yes?" he prompted. Karl rarely used his native Russian tongue. Unless of course he was being cute, or he was upset or flustered. He didn't have the sparkle in his blue eyes that would have indicated cute. The twitch at the corner of his mustache indicated upset.

It was as though he were biting his tongue, dying to say something, but bound by an invisible gag.

Dylan pulled the note out of his wallet. "This your calling card, Karl?"

Karl turned away. That wasn't like him. He prided himself on his notes of advice, always owned up to them. "I do recall that note, yes."

"And do you recall putting it in my jacket?"

"Maybe I made a mistake. I am an old man and the mind plays tricks at times."

Dylan snorted. "Pull the other leg, will you? Spill it, Karl. Is Whitney going to have my baby?"

"I honestly do not know." And that at least was the truth, Karl thought. She had not actually named Dylan as the father of her baby. For that matter, she had not actually admitted to the baby at all. But he'd seen the distress, the deep pain. He was ninety-nine percent sure, but not absolutely certain.

And he'd made a solemn promise. Though that promise hadn't had anything to do with not telling her whereabouts. He pushed the note back across the counter.

"I am not discussing this errant note with you, Dylan." Oh, the frustration on the boy's face! Brown eyes flashing, clenched jaw ticking, fingers balled into fists pressing the glass counter. Karl wasn't in any way concerned that Dylan would turn that anger on him. But he did feel bad for the young man.

He knew exactly how he felt—the uncertainty, the shock, the wondering, the feeling of one's world suddenly being snatch from beneath one's feet.

He hoped to God Dylan made the right decision now. Because Karl wasn't altogether certain he'd made the right decision all those years ago. And there was no going back now. No way to fix it. It was done. And he'd had to live with the pain, the bittersweet memories.

"Why can't you discuss this with me? It's your handwriting. You wrote the note."

"I might have made a mistake."

Dylan narrowed his eyes. Karl rarely made mistakes. "Are you going to tell me where she is?"

"Certainly. She is at the beach cottage. You remember the way?"

Of course he remembered the way.

THE BEACH HOUSE was a two-story structure painted robin's egg blue. In fact all the homes along this private stretch of beach had wood siding and gingerbread trim and looked as though they belonged in a giant Easter basket. Quaint porches spilling pots of flowers faced the narrow street crowded with cars.

Whitney didn't answer his knock, so he went around to the back of the house. This was where residents spent their time, anyway. The wood deck was resplendent with cozy patio furniture in a navy-and-white stripe. The sliding-glass door stood open, as did the gate that led from the patio down a set of steps onto the white sand beach.

And wouldn't you just know it, Dylan thought. There was Whitney, flirting with that blond surfer who owned more companies than Dylan could keep track of; the guy who had a crush on Whitney as big as the Pacific Ocean.

Jealousy slammed into him—which was perfectly ridiculous. After all, *he* was the one who'd come back to town engaged. He didn't have the right to get mad over who Whitney did or didn't flirt with.

Then again, she could very well be having his baby.

That gave him certain privileges, didn't it? If she was having his baby, he didn't want some other guy sniffing around. And that overly friendly neighbor was definitely sniffing, practically salivating like a starving dog.

Dylan pushed the gate wider and started down the steps, forgetting to take off his shoes until the sand slipping over the edge of his loafers reminded him of the oversight.

The sun was sinking low on the horizon, setting the sea on fire. A molten orange sunset painted the high, swirling clouds a vibrant peach against the turquoise sky. This was the time when it seemed the whole world held its breath, when change hovered, waited, suspended on the delicate fringes of dusk.

And as he'd known she would, Whitney stopped talking to what's-his-name and watched nature's splendor with awe. It was a beauty that one could never get tired of.

He shook his head, felt his lips curve up at the corners. Blondie was still talking, not even realizing he'd lost Whitney's attention to the sunset. Pity the guy didn't pay closer attention to the woman he was wooing. Then again, Pretty Boy was probably more interested in his oiled pecs than in detecting the in-attention or sadness in a woman's eyes.

And Dylan could just about lump himself in that same insensitive category—which upset him to no end. He'd been so caught up in his own woes, the company, the merger, he hadn't been as in-tuned to Whitney. Oh, he'd noticed something wrong, and to give him his due, he'd asked about it, been concerned. But he hadn't pushed hard enough; he'd given up too easily.

He wasn't going to make that mistake again.

He walked up behind her and put his hand on her shoulder. She jolted, whipped around.

Dylan's eyes narrowed and he frowned. Her face blanched and the scar over her lip whitened. When she swayed slightly, he stepped close, using his body to steady her. She had a headache coming on—one of her migraines, he suspected. He knew the signs. And he'd just helped it along by scaring the tar out of her.

"Sorry, Slim," he murmured, automatically reaching to the base of her neck, working his fingers gently into her skull. To the blond dude, he held out his hand. "Dylan Montgomery."

"Yeah, man, I remember."

"Hmm, I don't seem to recall *your* name." Oh, that was pretty low, never mind that he was operating on this weird jealousy. These Neanderthal tendencies that surfaced every time he was around Whitney lately were really getting out of hand.

Surfer Dude didn't seem to take offense, though. He grinned, his perfect teeth gleaming white in his tanned face. "Brett Coleman." He squeezed Dylan's hand a little harder and longer that necessary.

"Ah, Coleman surfboards, right?"

"Among other things." The tone was a challenge.

So, behind the innocent teeth was a bit of snap, Dylan mused. He'd have been happy to stand here for a while longer to see which one of them could growl the loudest, but he felt Whitney sag against him. He slipped his arm around her waist, tightened his hold.

Brett finally seemed to realize that she wasn't quite up to par. "Hey, are you all right, Whitney? You're looking a little pale."

Knowing she didn't like to talk when one of these headaches came on, Dylan started to answer for her.

She cut him off. "I'm fine, Brett. Just a bit tired."

"Is there anything I can do?" Coleman took a step closer.

Dylan all but stuck out his foot. "I'm here now. She'll be fine."

"Is that right, Whitney?" Brett asked, ignoring Dylan.

She gave a strained smile, nodded. "Thanks, Brett. Although it might not seem so, he is housebroken." She indicated Dylan with a nod of her head then winced. "Can I get back to you about the jazz concert?"

"Sure. I'll call you tomorrow."

Dylan wasn't liking the turn of this conversation. Making dates now?

He glanced down at Whitney and all his ugly thoughts vanished. Her eyes were mere slits, as though even the soft glow of dusk was too bright.

She was in bad shape and only holding on by a thread.

"Can you walk?" he asked softly, tightening his arm around her waist.

She nodded, put a hand to her temple.

"I can carry you."

"No," she whispered. "Just help me."

He knew she'd feel embarrassed if he picked her up, that she'd think everyone would be watching. And though he didn't give a damn what anybody else thought, he did care about Whitney's feelings.

Supporting her weight, he half lifted, half guided her back to the patio steps. To anyone who cared to look, they'd only appear like lovers clinging to one another, taking their sweet time about getting to the bedroom. In actuality, Whitney's vision was probably nonexistent by now.

He guided her around the outdoor table and chairs, through the open sliding-glass doors.

"Couch or bedroom?"

"Bed."

Now that they were inside, away from prying eyes, he bent, hooked his arm under her knees and lifted her. She didn't make a peep of protest. Her head rested on his shoulder, her eyes closed, her face pale as a ghost.

There wouldn't be answers to his questions tonight.

He laid her on the lemon-yellow quilt, tossed aside lacy pillows in poppy and blue—the inside decor was as colorful as the outside.

"Can you get undressed by yourself, or do you need help?" She'd changed out of the miniskirt since he'd seen her last, and now wore a pair of sweats that were soft from numerous washings.

"I'm fine."

He ran his hand over her back, to soothe, but it also told him she wasn't wearing a bra. So, okay, that caused his body to react, but it also assured him she wouldn't be too uncomfortable if she slept in her clothes.

"Where's your medicine?" he asked, keeping his voice soft.

"Just get me some Tylenol."

"Did you forget to bring your pills?"

She kept her eyes closed, gave a slight shrug.

"Changed purses again, huh?" She was always switching handbags and leaving something she just absolutely *had* to have in the other one. It's a wonder she could keep up with anything at all. And he loved to tease her about it.

"Guess it's a good thing I showed up, hmm? I'll run back to your house and get the pills and be back before you know it."

"No!" She bolted up in the bed, then clutched at her head and moaned.

"Hey, take it easy." He frowned, surprised by her outburst, and eased her back against the pillows. "We'll make do with some extra-strength Tylenol. If there's none around here, I've got some in the car."

"Kitchen cabinet next to the sink," she murmured weakly.

"Fine. You gonna stay put or do that jack-in-the-box routine again?"

She gave him his answer by curling into a ball.

He looked down at her for a moment, then made

his way to the kitchen. In a hurry to get to the pain medication, he didn't watch where he was going. His toe caught on the strap of her suitcase—which was still sitting in the entry hall. Her purse, resting atop the case, fell to the floor, spilling its contents all over the place.

He scooped up the leather bag, stuffed all manner of feminine paraphernalia back into the unzipped compartments. His hand landed on a prescription bottle. He read the label, and frowned.

Then everything within him went utterly, thoughtfully still.

She had her pain medication with her, after all.

But she hadn't wanted to take it.

Two and two was starting to add up. Her polite refusal to consume alcohol. Her vehement reaction when he'd offered to collect her prescription for her.

A pregnant woman wouldn't want to drink alcohol. Or take strong pain medications without consulting a doctor.

And he wondered if she *had* seen a doctor.

His emotions were all over the place. He touched his hip pocket where his wallet rested—where the note was tucked.

Until this moment he hadn't really thought about the actual truth—if there really was a baby. Hadn't believed it. Or maybe he'd been denying it.

But it didn't look as though denial would work anymore.

He ran cool tap water into a glass, found the bottle of Tylenol in the cupboard and carried both back to the bedroom.

Whitney had always been such a strong woman. She could give as good as she got, never asked for a handicap or special treatment. She was good-hearted, genuine through and through. She didn't complain, kept a stiff upper lip.

In fact, when she'd cut open her lip that time on the rocks, she'd shrugged it off, insisting she was fine, that they should just continue on with their day, not waste time worrying about a little blood.

Dylan'd had to practically toss her over his shoulder to get her to the doctor for stitches.

And because he was so used to that strength, it made him feel really helpless when she got one of these headaches. They zapped her, paralyzed her, incapacitated her. Drained every bit of strength out of her.

Here, she was vulnerable, and it showed.

He eased onto the side of the bed, slipped an arm under her shoulders, lifted her slightly. "Can you swallow these?"

She opened her lips as he placed a couple of the pills on her tongue, then held the glass to her mouth. She swallowed, whispered, "More."

"More pills? Are you sure?"

"Yes."

He complied, shook out two more and helped her swallow, then eased her back down and pushed his fingers through her hair, kneading her scalp.

"Yes or no?" he asked. Sometimes even the slightest touch would make the pain worse. He wanted to take care, to make it better, not worse.

"Yes," she said weakly, her voice trembly.

"Heck of a way to collect on these massages, Slim."

Even through the pain, Whitney felt little pinpricks of pleasure race up her spine, felt goose bumps raise the hair on her arms where she'd pushed up the sleeves of her sweatshirt. He massaged, stroked, petted, ran his fingertips lightly over her closed eyelids, her temple, her forehead, her ears, then back to the scalp, easing.

Tears leaked out of the sides of her eyes. She wasn't sure if they were more from physical or emotional pain.

"Shh," he whispered, easing down beside her, resting her against him, stroking away the moisture beneath her eyes, continuing his ministrations. "Shh, I've got you."

Whitney knew it would make the pain ten times worse if she gave in to the tears. But she couldn't seem to help it. His tenderness was her undoing.

She was simply distraught and trying valiantly not to show it. And when that happened, her body failed her, in the form of the migraines. In this she couldn't hide, couldn't be strong, couldn't pretend.

And Dylan knew that about her. He'd been through several of these episodes with her. He knew just what to do, just what to say, just how to touch, to soothe. He was so incredibly gentle, yet so masculine, so understanding—at times reminding her of a girlfriend, yet he was a guy, a really great guy.

This was the specialness she was so afraid of losing.

But right now her biggest worry had to do with Dylan's sudden appearance here. He'd followed her. Why? And Uncle Karl would have been the one to tell her whereabouts. Had he also gone back on his promise and told Dylan about the baby, too? She didn't think Uncle Karl would do that.

But something had prompted Dylan to seek her out

again so soon. And right now she wasn't in any shape to keep up the charade. She wasn't a hundred percent. And that's what it would take for her to evade. That's what it would take for her to smile through the pain, to convince him to go on with his life.

If he pushed now, she'd crumble.

And she'd very likely ruin his life.

The vise around her head squeezed harder, pulsing in time with the fierce pumping of her heart.

"Shh," Dylan whispered again. "You're tense, Slim. Relax. Let me take care of you. Sleep. I'll be here for you. Just let it go. Don't fight it. You don't have to be strong all the time."

There was an underlying tone that seemed to hold more meaning, but she just couldn't grasp it right now. So she concentrated on his hands, those wonderful hands, focused on his fingertips as he stroked her over and over, down her cheeks, over her eyelids, around the shell of her ear, kneaded her shoulders, her arms, then back up again to her head.

And the relaxation did come—in slow degrees. The pain was too intense for any more thought.

"Just relax, Slim."

His voice was hypnotic, as were his hands.

Dylan felt her muscles finally go lax, yet he still kept his hands moving, gently, absently. A glance at the bedside clock told him he'd been at it for more than an hour, but he didn't stop.

He knew what Whitney went through with these headaches. If she could fall into a deep enough sleep, she'd be fine. If she couldn't get to that healing place in slumber, the pain would hold on for days.

So he continued to stroke her, to make sure she

fell deeper and deeper. It tore him up to see her in pain.

She was so stubborn, and so headstrong. He wondered if she would even admit to the pregnancy, or if he'd have to pull the information out of her.

Why was she holding back this way? He didn't have any of the answers, but he would get them. Just as soon as she was up to it.

In the meantime he would stay—for as long as it took.

He eased off the bed and she didn't stir. Good. She was deeply asleep.

He went to retrieve her belongings from the entry hall before anybody else took a tumble. And that's when he noticed the rest of her things—the portable sewing machine, the bolts of vivid fabric, a fishing tackle chest filled with every sewing gadget known to man.

She'd been planning to stay for a while. Without letting him know.

He felt a pang, as though he'd been thrown to the wolves, left to fend for himself in this scary, uncertain time a mere week before his wedding, left adrift without the support of his best friend.

God, what was he thinking? He had a cryptic note burning a hole in his pocket, damning evidence that his best friend was having his baby. How could he even be thinking about marriage to anybody else?

Moving to the living room, he sat in a rainbow-sherbet-striped chair that faced the wall of glass, and propped his feet on an ottoman. He didn't bother to turn on any lights. His thoughts were best kept in the dark. Because they felt dark…and dangerous, and frustrating and scary as hell.

God, he was tired. Bone tired. He couldn't remember ever feeling this wrung out. And what must Whitney be feeling? Well, he knew. She was distraught, determined to go it alone.

And he was determined not to let her go it alone. They were friends, in this together.

Sure, it all appeared to be a mess right now. After all, he was supposed to be getting married in less than a week's time. But they'd figure something out.

He'd figure something out.

What, he wasn't sure.

With the hypnotic crash of phosphorus surf on glistening, moon-drenched sand, Dylan shut his eyes and his mind, letting the ocean sounds and the familiarity around him ease the edgy tension that had become such a part of him lately.

Chapter Eight

Whitney stretched gingerly beneath the bedcovers. Considering the acute agony she'd been in, she felt pretty good this morning—well, it was almost afternoon, she realized, glancing at the clock. The headache was gone; obviously it hadn't had the chance to get a really firm hold on her.

And that was thanks to Dylan. His massage had loosened the tension, put her into a healing sleep. And because she hadn't taken her high-powered prescription medication, she didn't feel sluggish and drugged out this morning.

Lemon sunlight poured through the windows and the smell of sea air bolstered her, as it always did. Whitney loved the ocean, the sight, the sound, the scents. A gull wheeled overhead, screeching its cry in search of food.

And Whitney realized she could use a little food, too.

Halfway through the living room, she stopped short. She could see the back of Dylan's head as he slouched in the upholstered writer's chair, his feet propped on the ottoman, his body facing the unobstructed view of the sand and ocean.

Had he slept there?

And was he still asleep?

She moved up beside him, glanced down. With the barest shift of his head, she realized that he was indeed awake. His brown eyes were intense, a bit troubled, very determined.

"Morning," she said.

He didn't speak. Just stared. She grew uncomfortable, shifted from foot to foot. Why did she suddenly feel so shy and awkward around him? This was awful, just the sort of thing she'd been afraid would happen. She didn't want to feel shy and awkward around Dylan. She wanted things back to the way they used to be.

Before he'd gotten engaged.

Before there was a baby.

Oh, that thought made her feel bad. She loved this baby already, wanted it with a fierceness that surprised her.

"Headache better?"

She nodded. "Thank you. You've still got the touch."

"We need to talk."

She glanced out the window, stalled and nearly screamed when his hands closed around her waist, pulled her right down on his lap.

"What in the world?"

"I'm not letting you avoid me this time. You sure that headache's all the way gone?"

"Yes, but—"

"Then talk to me, Slim." He shifted his hand to her belly, the warmth of his palm searing her, making her heart pound.

Her eyes snapped to his. Now she *really* felt awkward.

"You're going to have my baby, aren't you?"

She drew her lip between her teeth, the admission right there in her throat, aching to be set free, her stomach twisted into knots. It was too soon to say the words. She had it all planned. Wait. Stall. Don't rock the boat. Don't ruin his life.

He reached for her hand, hooked his pinky finger with hers, looked into her eyes.

It was her undoing. She couldn't lie anymore. She had to face this— Oh, she'd planned to face it anyway, it was just that now she'd be doing it a little sooner than she'd wanted.

"Yes."

"Why didn't you tell me? Why did you lie?"

"You're getting married, Dylan."

His brows lifted. "Are you kidding? This changes everything. I'll have to call it off because I can't—"

She scrambled off his lap, cutting him off in midsentence. "Don't you dare put that kind of guilt trip on me!"

"What?" Clearly astonished, he gaped at her.

"I'm no home-wrecker, Dylan. I like Cori. And furthermore, I'll not be the wobbly domino that causes the chain reaction fall of the Montgomery clan." If that merger didn't go through, Grace would lose her beautiful old Mediterranean estate and Candice would be turned out of her lovely cottage she'd made her own and was so proud of. The downfall of the town's founding family would be so very public, and dined on for years.

And Dylan...

Dylan would suffer the most.

He'd spent his life trying to please his father. To fail—even though it was inadvertently his dad's fault to begin with, and even though Randolph Sr. wasn't here to see it—would devastate him.

He might be able to hide from that truth in his quest to do the *right* thing by her, but she knew. She wouldn't let him make this sacrifice.

And it looked as if it was going to be a really tough battle. They were both stubborn people. And this was definitely a clash of wills.

He stood, looking as fierce as she—more so. She almost took a step back. This was a side of Dylan she rarely saw, the raw anger.

"Why don't you let me worry about the company, hmm?"

"I'd be happy to, provided you aren't hell-bent on throwing it away on a whim."

"You call having a baby a whim?"

"No, but *you're* not having a baby, *I* am. And it's my responsibility, not yours."

A muscle jumped in his jaw. He shoved his hands deep into his pockets, as though to keep them from reaching for her throat. "I'm going to pretend you didn't say that."

Lord, she was making a hash out of this. The aim was to convince him to look at the big picture, not goad him into acting on ego. Or on honor and integrity.

Because there was one thing she could not take with regard to Dylan. She could not take it if she knew she only got him because of the baby. If she knew she'd trapped him. And in trapping him, had caused his entire life to crumble.

Maybe they could get by for a while, kid themselves that all would be well, that love would make the world go around.

But he didn't love her like that...enough to make the world go around. Oh, he loved her—that was a given because of their friendship, their history together, their closeness. But he wasn't burning, *in* love with her, the unconditional, air-you-breathe, forever-and-a-day, I-gotta-have-you-touch-you-see-you-kiss-you-love-you kind of love.

The kind of love she wanted.

She didn't want to be second in his life. She'd rather be his *best* friend than his shotgun bride.

The friendship was one he'd *chosen*.

The marriage would be one he'd been pressured into—because of a baby.

Actually it was probably a blessing that the marrying kind of love wasn't a paramount issue between them. Then it really would make this whole mess all the more bittersweet.

Because to act on that love would cause severe, irreversible consequences. People would lose their jobs, their homes, their livelihoods, their respect and standing in the community.

And watching that happen, especially for a man as sensitive as Dylan, would crush his spirit.

No, she couldn't let that happen. And she had to convince him of it.

"Dylan, I'm not trying to be nasty. I would never keep your child from you. You can have liberal visitation rights, daily if you want...anything you want."

He turned to her, watched her for a long, nerve-racking moment. Then he asked very, very quietly, "What if I want *you?*"

Her heart actually leaped, stung. A couple of weeks ago she would have latched on to that question, done everything in her power to make it happen, to hook him before he had a chance to have second thoughts.

But that was before she'd known about his engagement, about his company's problems, about the insurmountable stakes riding on this merger.

The sadness that welled nearly made her sway.

She took a breath, shook her head and pasted a smile on her face. "Don't be ridiculous, Dylan. We're just friends."

"You're making me mad." He jerked his hands out of his pockets, raked his fingers through his short hair. "Yes, we're friends." His voice rose. "And we've been lovers." Now he was nearly shouting. "And we're having a baby!"

"And you're getting married next weekend," she shouted right back. "And if you don't, you'll blow a billion dollar deal!"

"I told you—"

"Damn it, I *know* what you told me. I'm not letting you mess up your life. And I don't want to talk about it anymore. I know you, Dylan. You're honorable and noble and have integrity that's an ocean deep. And I refuse—do you hear me?—I *refuse* to snatch some guy away from another woman just because I was too stupid to think about birth control. I can take full responsibility for my life and I intend to. Nobody's going to sacrifice for me like Uncle Karl did. Nobody. I don't want to get married. I want to be a fashion designer. Now you can be my friend and back off, or get the hell out of my house!"

Astonished by her outburst, he stared, then opened

his mouth to refute a few of those statements. But she obviously wasn't through yet.

"Why can't we just go on like we always have? You'll still be in our lives—me and the baby's—just like you've always been. Except for the, uh, sex thing, I mean."

"I *liked* the sex thing."

She turned her eyes to the ceiling, swallowed. He could see her battle with her emotions, which she was only holding on to by a thread; see the tears that welled because she obviously thought he wasn't paying attention, that he was discounting her feelings and wishes.

He pulled her to him, pressed his lips against her hair. "Okay, okay. Have it your way. We're best friends and I'm still getting married this weekend." If possible, she went even more rigid in his arms.

"I don't need your sarcasm."

"I know. I'm sorry. I'm not—I didn't mean to be."

Well, hell, Dylan thought, he wasn't making a bit of sense. He'd never seen Whitney so worked up, so damned close to the edge. And he'd never seen her lie through her teeth any smoother. In one breath she was kicking him out the door and in the next her eyes and her tone begged him to stay, to ignore her words and just stay. He didn't even think she realized what she was doing.

Surely it wasn't good for either her or the baby to get this distraught.

He shifted his lips to her temple, absently kneaded her shoulders. She had a point about the business, and that dilemma was going to take some thinking about. There were others to consider—his employees, his family. Jobs were at stake. Homes were at stake. The development of his dream—the lasers—was at stake. He had one month to satisfy the balloon payment.

But Whitney was having his baby. That should be the most important thing.

He couldn't *make* her change her mind, and that's what really had him twisted into knots. They should be putting their heads together, trying to come up with a solution.

No. That was *his* responsibility. He realized how much he'd come to rely on her, to count on her to be there to talk over his problems with, to bounce ideas off. This time, though, he couldn't.

Because she'd dug in her heels.

Hell, she'd just told him to back off or get out. He'd always loved her headstrong stubbornness, gotten a kick out of it. Then again, her stubbornness had never affected him on such a personal level before.

But he would do as she asked—or try to, at least. And in the meantime he had less than a week to try to change her mind. She accused him of being the noble one, when in fact it was she who was the queen of that particular trait.

Right now, though, the tension in the room was way too thick. He needed to diffuse it.

He cupped her cheek, felt a kinetic jolt of pure, exhilarating sensation shoot through him. *Friends only, my foot!*

He wanted this woman, this *friend,* with a fierceness that nearly dropped him to his knees.

He loved her.

But that still didn't get either of them out of this quagmire. And he didn't think he could make such a heavy decision—regarding the future of his company, the future of his family—unless he had Whitney's support and cooperation.

And he wasn't going to get that by upsetting her.

His only hope was to show her what they had together.

"I really wish you wouldn't kick me out," he said.

"Dylan, you're getting married—"

"Come on, Slim. Take pity on me. Cori's wrapped up in her work and she's not even taking any time off. There's nothing for me to do—I wouldn't be hanging out with her, anyway. Mrs. Spencer is taking care of all the fussy details." God, he'd need to do something about those two things soon—Cori and the wedding her mother was planning—but right now his brain was working on overload. One thing at a time, he told himself, and the thing right now was to concentrate on Whitney.

"What about the company problems?"

"Believe it or not, this week is like a freeze frame. Everything is on hold until after next Saturday. And what's not on hold, Mark's handling. So, you see? I've got idle time on my hands, my life's upside down and I could use a…a friend." *Both* their lives were upside down.

She stepped back a pace and narrowed her eyes. He let her go.

"Are you trying to push my sympathy buttons?"

"Yes. Is it working?"

She smiled, really smiled this time. "It could be."

He loved the way her green eyes shimmered when something—or someone—pleased her. "So, I can stay?"

"Well, I could use a houseboy." She squeezed his

biceps, hummed an approving noise in the back of her throat.

Dylan laughed. "What are 'houseboy' duties?"

"For starters, unloading my van. I didn't have a chance to do it yesterday."

"What's in the van?"

"My sewing stuff."

"Your sewing stuff's in the hall. I already tripped over it."

"That's just the machine and a few bolts of fabric."

"Something tells me that van's stuffed to the panels."

She winked at him. "As always, your intuition is right on. I'll make you a deal. I'll fix us something to eat so when you're done you can revive those weak muscles."

"You think my muscles are gonna be weak?"

"Yep. And I won't have you crying foul if I beat you at badminton."

"You've never beaten me at badminton."

"I have, too."

"When?"

"When I was sixteen."

"Now, come on. That wasn't a fair-and-square win, and you know it."

"It was, too."

"Your bathing suit top came untied."

"So. A true athlete perseveres through any surprises or upsets. Just because you got flashed isn't an excuse for losing the game. Now, are you gonna empty my van or should we arm wrestle?"

"Maybe we should. Because according to you,

when I'm done these arms are gonna be real wimpy.''

She gave him a shove in the direction of the garage. "Get. I'll be in the kitchen if anything's too heavy for you."

He shook his head. "You're such a smart aleck."

"Yeah, and you love it."

The minute she said the words, she regretted them. Time seemed to stand still. Oh, this wasn't going to work. Here she'd just agreed to let him stay and now she was going to have to watch every little word she said, every little innuendo. Ideally, what he was asking for was a week spent just like they used to—playing and squabbling and talking and just...being.

That was going to be real tricky with this sexual current flowing between them like a live wire.

"I'll, uh, just toss together something for brunch."

Whirling, she fled to the kitchen. The window looked out over the deck onto the sandy beach. She saw Brett Coleman jog into the waves, toss his surfboard in front of him and follow it belly-first. His powerful swimmer's arms gave nice definition to the sleek black wet suit as he paddled through the breakers.

She'd have to think about that invitation he'd extended for the jazz festival. That was going to be a bit touchy with Dylan here. Even through the pain of an encroaching migraine, she'd sensed the tension between those two men, had felt a little like a bone being tugged between rival dogs.

She shook her head. This was ridiculous. Dylan was still just a friend. The father of her baby, true, but just a friend. They weren't getting married. He didn't have a claim on her. She was free to date other men.

More free than *he* was to date other women, she realized on a pang.

Lord, Cori Spencer was a good sport and all, but Whitney had to wonder how the other woman would truly feel about Dylan spending the week here with her.

Then again, maybe it was her own magnification of things. Her own feelings, because she really, *really* wanted to go to bed with him again.

The thought stunned her. "Oh, for Pete's sake."

She spun away from the window, opened the refrigerator and took out some apples, cheese and melons. She'd zap some bran muffins in the microwave and they'd have a light but healthy brunch.

She ran water over a shiny red apple, dried it with a paper towel and gripped the stem, not even realizing what she was doing until she'd turned it four revolutions and given a tug.

Her hands stilled as memory coalesced—young girls, twisting the stems of their apples to determine the identity of their one and only true love…the boy they'd marry.

And Whitney had rarely twisted her apple more than four revolutions. D for Dylan. And on the fourth turn, just to hedge the odds, she'd always given a slight tug, an extra little bit of help—as she'd just done.

She stared at the apple in her hand, and at the stream of running water from the tap she hadn't shut off.

There was a time when she'd liked a boy—Wes was his name—but the apple stems had never made that many revolutions, no matter how gently she'd twisted—or how cleverly she'd cheated with half or quarter turns.

Funny how she'd remember that now. Back then, after Wes had kissed Lisa Tallan behind the portables at school, Whitney had been glad the darn apple stem had never made it to his initial. He'd been a dweeb, anyway.

But Dylan...Dylan was a friend, a constant. He was *hers*.

She shook her head, tossed the apple stem down the garbage disposal, picked up the next apple, and when she found herself twirling that stem, too, she hissed out a breath, grabbed a paring knife out of the drawer and savagely sliced right down the middle of the crisp fruit.

"It doesn't mean anything," she said out loud. "It's just like that step-on-a-crack singsong or the Macarana dance. Once you get it in your head, you can't get it out."

"Get what out?"

She whirled around, the knife gripped in her hand.

Dylan held up a headless mannequin like a shield. "We're unarmed."

She looked down at the knife she held like a weapon, then back at him, tucking her lips between her teeth to keep from laughing at the comically stunned expression on his face as he peeked from behind the dummy. "If you keep sneaking up on people that way, you'll have to take the consequences."

"I'll remember that. And the dummy and I thank you for not jumping the gun—or the knife, rather. So, what can't you get out of your head?"

"That Macarana song."

He groaned, propped the mannequin in the corner of the breakfast nook by the bay window. "Do me a favor and keep it to yourself, would you?"

"Ah, now I know your weakness. If I want to get to you, I'll just start singing."

"And you'll find yourself gagged."

"I can still hum."

"You're a menace."

"Yep. And you're looking as though you need something else to do."

"I don't remember you being such a slave driver."

"Sure you do. Grab another knife and start slicing." She indicated a cantaloupe and a block of cheese with the tip of her knife.

He scooted her aside and washed his hands at the sink. "How the heck did you cram *all* that stuff in your van?"

"I've got some great neighbors. They helped."

Just then he looked through the window and spotted Brett surfing a nice size wave. "I suppose these neighbors were male?"

She grinned. "Guys aren't the only ones with claim to muscles. Teresa and Sam and I managed together." Teresa Longford, a single mom and watercolor artist lived across the street from Whitney's house. Sam, Teresa's sixteen-year old daughter, was Whitney's biggest fan. Tall and sleek as a gazelle, she was always thrilled to be one of the first to model a Whitney original.

Dylan tucked away his green-eyed monster. Had he always been this jealous? If he thought hard, looked back on all the times he and Whitney had commiserated over their relationships with others, he could recall feeling a certain tightening around the heart, a clench in the gut when she became close to another guy. And he recalled feeling a sense of relief when she and the flavor of the month went their separate ways.

Why hadn't he ever thought about that before now? Realized it until now?

That was significant.

They mixed up a bowl of fruit, a plate of cheese, and Whitney nuked some bran muffins from the local bakery. He recognized the packaging.

"We make a good team," he commented, setting mugs on the table.

"That's because we've known each other for so long."

He grabbed the coffeepot, hovered over her cup. "Should you be drinking coffee?"

"Beats me. I've never been pregnant before. I don't know the rules."

"Seems I heard something about caffeine being iffy. Suppose we should chance it?"

Whitney rolled her eyes. "What do you mean, *we?* And I don't think one cup will hurt. Besides, if I don't have at least a *little* caffeine in my system, I'll be face-first on the table by noon."

He still paused without pouring. "I don't know—"

She tipped his hand, causing coffee to splatter onto the table's white inlaid tile. "Don't be a fussbudget."

"Fine. But we're going to buy a book."

"Sit down and eat." She tossed a napkin over the liquid mess, went to the cupboard to retrieve another, distancing herself from both him and the uncomfortable subject of what was good or bad for pregnant women. And the *last* thing she needed was for him to buy a book.

Her goal was to make it through the rest of the week with little or no mention of the baby, to turn back the clock and enjoy one another just as they used to. To forget the problems, both his and hers.

And if she truly believed that was an attainable goal, then it was painfully obvious she'd taken a dangerous detour into fairyland.

Sitting at the table, she toyed with her meal and couldn't help watching him as he ate. The man as a whole was an absolute feast for the senses.

He still had on the same clothes he'd worn yesterday, dark gray slacks and a black shirt. Traces of his cologne lingered, mingling with the scent of warm bran muffins and fruit. He didn't have the perfect face of a Ken doll—there were creases in his forehead and wrinkles by his eyes, character lines that testified to laughter.

Dylan always said a man's gotta laugh otherwise he'll cry. She figured it was really tough on him, growing up with such a bull-headed, loudly opinionated man like Randolph, especially for a guy whose emotions and sensitivities ran deep and wide.

Needing a distraction from going down that particular path, Whitney grabbed her sketchbook and began drawing as she nibbled on apple slices and picked at a muffin.

In lieu of a floral centerpiece, a squatty crystal vase held an array of colored pencils and markers. She reached for a persimmon-hued shading pen.

Silverware tinkled and the table wobbled.

Dylan grabbed his coffee cup with one hand and her knee with the other.

She glanced up sharply, her heart pumping, the heat of his palm searing her, thrilling her. Lord, she wasn't going to survive the week.

Taking a breath, she tried for a casual smile. "Sorry."

He leaned forward, thank God he removed his hand. "What's this?" He turned the sketch pad so he could get a better look.

"A formal gown."

"I can see that. What's the baby doing there?"

She laughed a little self-consciously, an emotion she rarely felt when it came to her designs. "It's just something that came to me—a quilted satin baby sling to match the ball gown. It's for those black tie to-dos where children are welcome." She perused the design, liking the simple lines.

"Square-cut neck," she explained as though he wasn't already looking at the drawing. "Wide straps, fitted bust, empire waist, a soft, floor-length flow of matte silk held away from the body just slightly by a padded slip."

"Mmm, I see. Innocence. But this is a formal affair, a see and be seen. Why not go for sexy, clingy?"

"Because she's just had a baby. We want to look dynamite, yet camouflage any body flaws. Besides, the flame color and low neck will have every man in the room panting."

"I don't know, Slim. With a baby hanging around her neck? If this is black tie, how come she wants to bring the kid? Doesn't she want a night out alone?

And does such an affair even exist? A fancy outing where you bring the little ones?''

"Of course. Think about celebrity's babies. The privileged. Money talks. Whether there's an invitation or not, those children often show up. Might as well have them dressed for the occasion."

"I don't think I'd want the baby at the fancy dinner."

"So what are you going to do? Hire a baby-sitter?"

"Are you kidding? Mom would kill me."

She almost added that Uncle Karl would have a similar reaction. She realized what they were doing. Talking as though they were parents. As though *they* would be the beautiful couple going on the date.

But that wasn't so.

His *wife* would be the one to accompany him.

"It was just an idea. Nothing real." She shut the sketchbook with a snap. "I need some fresh air."

Chapter Nine

Dylan hopped and skipped, trying to get his shoes and socks off, his pant legs rolled up and still keep up with Whitney. He needed to retrieve the gym bag with his extra clothes from the car. He wasn't dressed for beach strolling or merchandise hauling.

"Wait up, Slim." She was already down the stone steps and onto the sand. He went through the gate with visions of breaking his neck on the sandy stairs as he hurried after her. Well, that would be one way to solve the wedding thing.

She turned, shaded her eyes with her hand, and grinned at his goofy near-slide down the steps. Despite a slight embarrassment that he was less than suave and in control, he couldn't help but admire her sassy smile. With Whitney, laughter always won out. No matter what.

Except for, of course, that one time when she was fifteen. He'd been in a foul mood. She'd needed a shoulder to cry on. He'd told her to get a grip, been insensitive to her needs. She'd fallen apart on him then. And it had been awful. Just awful.

He didn't like to think about it. So he focused on the sexy curve of her lips.

He'd like to kiss that mouth. And wouldn't she be stunned if he followed through on his desire.

He reined in those thoughts. "Where are we going in such a hurry?"

"Just for air. A walk. I didn't know you wanted to come or I'd have waited. Those five years you have on me are beginning to show."

"Excuse me?" Appalled, he realized he was actually insulted.

She laughed harder, hooked her arm through his, and dug her toes in the sand. "You're so easy to ruffle, Dyl."

"And you're a brat."

And that's what you love about me. He waited for her to say it. Any other time she would have. Just another of the changes that was really starting to bug him.

By the week's end, hopefully all would be right again.

Well, it would be a while before things were actually *right*. There was the matter of his company's stock falling, people depending on him, a baby about to be born in six or seven months' time. Hell, he had a fiancée that he kept forgetting about, knew he needed to deal with.

There were so many things running around in his head that he just wanted to shut down—to check out of the rat race for a while.

He didn't want to think. He just wanted to *be*. With Whitney.

He saw good old Coleman still sitting like a crow on his surfboard, waiting for a decent wave to carry him to shore.

A sharp twinge of jealousy pierced him. Dylan

didn't want to share, didn't want to take the chance of the other man interrupting or intruding on his time with Whitney.

"Race you to the bay." He took off, knowing she'd pick up the challenge. Too late, he remembered about the baby. Maybe she shouldn't be racing like an idiot across the sand. He hesitated, truly worried, and it was just the edge she needed to overtake him, to stick out her tongue and charge right on past.

"Wait!"

Her laughter trailed on the breeze. He took off again, gaining on her, but not enough. It was hell on his overworked and underused libido to watch her shapely backside, to watch the muscles in her legs flex, her gluts tighten as her toes dug into the sugary sand, gripped, pushed off, propelled her forward. She was a superb athlete, a pleasure to watch. Her chestnut hair lifted in the breeze and bounced against her shoulders and back.

He was close. Really close. Almost level now, gaining. He'd take her, pass her. She wouldn't gloat over this. Besides, he deserved to win. He'd been ahead before he'd tripped himself up with his own thoughts.

Suddenly she pulled up short, stuck out her foot, chortled in laughter as he went sailing to the sand. He tucked, rolled and lay there winded.

The sky was blue with great white puffy clouds, a beautiful spring day. He saw it through the slits in his eyes and decided to play possum.

He heard her panting as she came to stand over him, heard her laughter change, die off.

"Dylan?" Tentative. "Dylan?" More worry now. "Oh, no, Dylan, you're hurt, I'm so—"

Lightning quick, he snagged her wrist, yanked her down, broke her fall with his body, and rolled her beneath him, hooking a leg over her thighs.

Her shriek ended on another laugh. "You faker."

"You cheat."

"I didn't cheat!"

"Yes, you did. You distracted me and got the jump. Then when I was just about to make up the time, you deliberately tripped me."

"True about the deliberate tripping. But I'm not responsible for your distraction."

And talk about being distracted. Her chest heaved from the exertion of the run, her breasts pressing against his chest with each breath she took. He was half over her, the lower part of his body aligned in a way that would make a dead man sit up and take notice.

Her green eyes widened and her breathing changed. Her gaze shifted to his mouth, then back to his eyes. She was thinking about kissing him. So much for just friends.

He was making progress.

Because he was feeling so smug, he rolled off her—and grinned when he saw the confusion in her green eyes, the disappointment, and the way she valiantly tried to hide both of those emotions.

He turned so he wouldn't give himself away. Because he was really hard. And he wanted really bad. But in good time.

All in good time.

"How's that for fresh air?" he asked. It occurred to him that he was starting to feel that caveman stuff again, was a mere breath away from beating his chest. Damnedest thing.

"A little more strenuous than I had in mind."

He stood, held out a hand, helped her to her feet, brushed the sand from her backside.

She squeaked and leaped away from him.

His brow rose. "Problem?"

"I think there might be. What in the world has gotten into you?"

"I don't know what you're talking about."

"Those...those looks, and the touches. That thing you did looking at my mouth."

"You were the one doing the hungry-mouth look, not me."

"I was not."

"Was, too." He grinned. Everything with her was a challenge. Even a verbal by-play was something to be bested.

She was fairly flustered right now, though. That was the only reason he could come up with for how easily she conceded the battle, how she turned away, brushed at her own backside, gave him a warning look, then gazed back out at the sea.

He slung an arm around her shoulders, kept it there even when she tried to shrug it off. He would wear her down before the week was out. What they'd taken for granted as friendship had evolved into much, much more. And she was going to admit it.

Regardless of the baby, there was something really good between them.

He ignored the anxiety that built in his chest, ignored the voice that nagged at him, questioned if he was doing the right thing. By dragging her into the middle of his life's upheaval, could he somehow end up hurting her more?

And what if he lost it all? Was there enough in

his personal accounts and investments to take care of her? Of the baby? Of his mother and sister?

He didn't have any of the answers, and that made him all the more uptight. The only thing he knew for certain was that he wanted to hold on to Whitney. To hold on tight.

They walked in silence for a while, occasionally stopping to pick up a shell, nearly tripping one another trying to dodge some of the faster moving waves that rushed onshore.

The sand was powdery white and free of debris and glass. This was a private beach and the residents took pride in it. They reached the cove where the water was clear and blue-green, lapping gently onshore. Driftwood was piled on the sand, helped along by the local kids who built forts and lean-tos and teepees out of the bleached wood.

Here, the roar of the sea was muted by the surrounding grass-covered cliffs and rocky caves. Whitney dug her toes into the wet sand, stooping to pick up a hollowed out piece of wood that would make a perfect pretend canoe for the children who came to play. She set it aside where the sea wouldn't sweep it away, and stared out at the clear depths of the gentle surf.

"This is what paradise would look like," she said softly.

"Mmm-hmm." Funny how he'd never really considered paradise, or what it would be like.

"Dylan?"

"Hmm?"

"Can I ask you something?"

"Sure, Slim."

She was silent for so long, he'd about decided she'd changed her mind. Then, "Do you love her?"

Oh, God, how many times in the past had she asked him those same four words? Every time she'd counseled him on one of his many relationships, he realized. And those four words were always what put things in perspective for him, showed him that the relationship wasn't going anywhere, couldn't compete, would never hold his attention as work or friends or family could.

As Whitney could.

"I care about her."

"*Could* you? Love her."

"I respect her. I'm fond of her." It occurred to him that they both seemed reluctant to say Cori's name. He glanced down at Whitney. "Don't give me that look. I'm trying to answer honestly here. And it's tough. I'd never planned to marry, never even thought about it until this merger thing."

He stopped, held her gaze, said softly, "I could marry you, though."

"Don't start."

"Okay, but I really don't want to talk about Cori."

"That's a pretty crummy way to be five days before the ceremony."

"It's not as if Cori's going to any trouble to spend time with me, you know. And I really don't want to talk about this." Shame swamped him, making his words terse, almost uncaring. Shame that he'd actually let himself get engaged to Cori Spencer, that he'd compromised to such an extent for the company.

Shame that he kept forgetting about the woman he'd agreed to marry. And acute guilt and confusion over how he was going to get out of the whole mess without causing great hurt and ruination of lives.

Whitney slipped her hand into his and gave it a squeeze. She could see the confusion in his eyes, feel his tension.

"Okay. So how come you never thought about marriage?" This subject was about to kill her, but Whitney pursued it anyway. Dylan needed to talk, needed a friend to understand, to help him understand. If she could do that for him, help him see his duty, look deep into his heart and find a way to accept, it would be worth the pain.

Because she certainly didn't want to see him hurting. And she knew it was imperative that he save the company from ruin. If marriage came with the merger—was required—he needed to accept it, to come to terms, to find a way to make peace, to be happy.

Dylan deserved to be happy.

She wanted that for him at least.

"Work's always been my bride. Before Dad died, I was working like a fiend to prove something, I think. Then afterward, well, I felt relieved that he wasn't there breathing down my neck. That's pretty bad, huh?"

"No. You're human, Dyl."

"Yeah, well, me and my humanity felt guilty for being relieved after he was gone, for feeling a sense of freedom, as though a weight had been lifted from my shoulders. But then I was working toward something new, something all mine."

"The lasers."

He nodded. "Now I'm just working to keep it all from turning to dust."

"And what does that have to do with your views on marriage—or previous views, I should say."

"Most of the women I've hooked up with couldn't put up with my single-minded dedication to the company, and that was always fine with me. The hours I put in at work consume me, leave little time to cater to a relationship." And when he'd had free time, he'd wanted to spend it with friends or family—Jack, Mom and Candice, Karl...Whitney.

It always came back to Whitney.

He was a fool for not seeing that sooner.

Would William Spencer have insisted on such archaic terms for the merger if Dylan had been involved with someone else? With Whitney?

Had he just been taking the easy way out to go back to Spencer after he'd found out what dire straits the company had fallen into? To agree to the deal that he'd originally passed on three months ago? If the offer hadn't been on the table, would he have found another avenue to pull the fat out of the fire?

But he hadn't thought about any of that. Whitney had been out of sight and out of mind—probably a deliberate mind block because of the shock of what had happened between them, then the added blow of her telling him it didn't mean anything, that it was only a fluke, a furthering of her education. His ego had been dented, for sure, but still, how could he have dismissed her so easily?

And had he?

Obviously not. Not the way his senses had all but stood on end and sang the second he'd laid eyes on her at the engagement party.

Hardly realizing that they'd done so, they had headed back toward the beach house. Right in front of Whitney's porch, a volleyball net had been erected.

Brett Coleman and a few of the other neighbors were gearing up for a game. The surfer grinned when he saw Whitney, his teeth white in his tanned face.

It annoyed Dylan that the other man all but ignored him.

"Hey, Whitney, you're just in time for a game." He finally glanced at Dylan. "You, too, Montgomery. That is, if you don't mind messing up your clothes."

He probably looked pretty ridiculous on the beach, with the butterscotch sun shining hot overhead, and him standing here in a black Donna Karan shirt and three-hundred-dollar pants with the cuffs rolled up to his shins.

Whitney, barefoot, in shorts and a skimpy T-shirt was dressed for the game. But Dylan didn't want to take the time to get his gym bag out of the car.

Brett Coleman would just love the opportunity to get the jump on him.

Dylan winked at Brett, reached for the buttons of his shirt. "Don't worry about it, Coleman. I've got a good dry cleaner."

Whitney froze right where she was, unable to drag her eyes away from Dylan. He'd peeled off his shirt, tossed it aside. For a man who worked in an office, he had some nice color to that glorious chest.

Her mouth went dry and her arms trembled. She remembered a scene from a movie—jet jockeys on a beach in a sweaty game of volleyball, shirtless, one of them wearing long pants, his chest a sculpted work of art—like Dylan's.

She watched as he leaned over to roll his pant

cuffs another turn. So intent, so focused on the sight of his body, she leaned, too, as though her gaze were attached by a string that tugged her right along with his movements.

Bent over, he turned his head, looked right at her, grinned—that irresistible, sly half grin that all but shouted, "Yeah, I'm trouble, but you gotta love me anyway."

She jerked upright, appalled by her panting behavior, horrified that he'd actually caught her at it. Dylan was a sexy, sexy man and he knew it.

To cover her reaction to him, she fell back on competitiveness with a touch of orneriness.

She caught the ball Brett tossed her, jogged over to his side of the net and nearly laughed at the way Dylan's brows slammed down. Well, if he'd expected her to be on his team, that was pure silliness. This was competition. War.

He met her at the center of the net. "You're gonna be on *his* team?"

"Make you nervous?"

"As a matter of fact, yes."

"I love it when a man admits that I'm better at a game than him."

"That's not what I was admitting."

"No? Then I'll be a distraction to you?"

She saw his lips twitch. "As long as you don't flash your chi-chis, I think we'll be okay."

She laughed. "Deal. Beside, be a sport, Dyl. If you and I paired up, we'd win hands down and it would be a really dull game. Because next to me, pal, you're second best at this game."

"We'll just see who's second best."

He jogged back to the serving corner of their

makeshift court, trying not to notice the way Whitney's breasts bounced as she danced on the sand, warming up her muscles.

If he made a single shot, he'd be lucky.

There was a perky blonde on his team, wearing a really tiny bikini, the kind that ran right up the center of her rear, showing off both tanned globes. The guy in him automatically looked, appreciated and reacted.

The volleyball conked him on the head.

He jerked his gaze, saw Whitney's scowl, knew instinctively she'd been the one to lob the ball. Ah, so she could get jealous, too.

He grinned, shrugged. "Sorry," he mouthed.

The little blonde glanced over her shoulder, giving him a flirty smile. He raised his brows, sent it right back to her.

Then he had to get serious. Because Whitney was going all out. Soon the game became a war between just the two of them. Neither bothered to set up the ball to their teammates. Instead they scrambled across the sand, left-to-right, diving, leaping, sliding.

He had sand down his pants, across his sweaty chest. Whitney hadn't hit the ground once.

That annoyed him. He was out of breath.

She was grinning.

He slammed the ball, sent it sailing to the left front corner. She was at the right far edge. She charged forward, tripped her teammate, dove for the ball, her hands clasped, wrists outward.

He saw the fall coming, and regretted the sneaky move. Damn it, a woman in her delicate condition shouldn't be playing such a strenuous game! And she definitely shouldn't be doing belly flops on the sand! What had he been thinking?

He leaped forward, slid beneath the net, maneuvered himself right under her, broke her fall, rolled with her in the sand, ended up with her lush body on top of his, straddling him, aligned so intimately he went hard in a millisecond.

Her hands were on his chest, her hair hanging around them like a curtain.

He couldn't help himself. He reached up, cupped the back of her neck, and pulled her lips down to his, tasting, exploring…savoring.

Salty.

Perfect.

His.

Whitney closed her eyes. She wasn't sure when exactly she'd stopped breathing. The sun beat against her back. Sweat trickled between her breasts. Her fingers flexed against Dylan's muscled chest.

His lips were soft and firm, his body beneath hers hard.

Very hard.

And she was straddling him.

In front of an audience.

She pulled back, tugged against his restraining hold, placed both hands on his chest and pushed. That wedged her more snugly against his arousal.

"Might not be such a good idea to stand up right now," he murmured, his brown eyes hot with desire yet sparkling with devilish lights.

She didn't know if she could speak, but gave it a try anyway. "Seems to me that's more your problem than mine."

"True. But you're a pal and wouldn't want to see me embarrassed, right?"

Whitney knew darn well he wouldn't be embarrassed by his body's reaction to her. But she would. Well, at least she'd feel a bit awkward.

She glanced up, saw Brett watching them with a resigned, friendly look on his face. Why in the world couldn't she have fallen in love with somebody like him?

She looked back at Dylan. "What the devil were you doing?"

"Kissing you."

"Before that."

"Catching you," he said softly, brushing away a strand of hair that clung to her damp cheek.

His tone and his eyes told her his meaning went much deeper than the literal interpretation. Her heart wanted to cling; her head knew better. "I didn't need catching."

"You were about to fall on your stomach. That wouldn't be good for the baby."

"I wouldn't have landed on my stomach if you hadn't tangled yourself with me. I'd have only gone as far as my knees."

"Looked like you were on the verge of a belly flop to me."

His concern was touching. She didn't want it to be. "Guess you need to get your eyes checked, old man. You're not seeing well."

"Old man, huh?" He bucked his hips, just a bit, to let her know he was still aroused and was plenty young enough for whatever she could think up.

"I was speaking about your vision."

"It's twenty-twenty, and I know what I saw, Slim. You were in trouble."

She shrugged. "Maybe. I hadn't intended to trip over Sally's feet." She eased back to his thighs, glanced down at his belt, the way his dress pants rode low on his waist, below his belly button. She stopped her gaze from going any farther south and forced it in the opposite direction. Dark hair arrowed upward, fanned out across his chest. Right where her hands were planted.

No matter where she looked, something made her think of sex. She wondered if this flood of hormones would continue for the next seven and a half months. If so, she was gonna be in big trouble.

"Are you two going to get back to the game any-time soon?" Brett asked with a slight snap to his tone.

She saw Dylan's devilish smile and suspected he was thinking about a completely different kind of game—a game she didn't dare try to win!

DYLAN WENT TO THE MARKET to pick up some steaks for dinner. He'd promised not to be any trouble if she would let him stay the week and he'd meant it. That included meals, too. He would do the cooking, or take her out.

He made a forty-minute detour to the estate to pick up extra clothes, and was thankful that he'd breezed in and out without being stopped by any of the family. Mom and Candice had gone dress shopping. Jack still wasn't around, and neither was Mark.

A copy of the *Wall Street Journal* had been tucked on top of his briefcase—left there by Mark, no doubt. Two of his competitors had merged. That would put even more of a squeeze on Montgomery Industries.

He wanted to strangle his father for putting every-one in this position. He had the most overpowering urge to walk away from it all, wondered if he had the guts. He glanced around the mausoleum of a house. How long could he hang on? Would William Spencer pull the plug if Dylan backed out of the marriage deal? And Cori…God, she'd agreed to the marriage—not for love, but she had her reasons. What was all this going to do to her life?

How had things gotten so out of hand?

He dialed Cori's number from his cell phone, dread making his palms sweat. While he listened to the tinny rings, he picked up his briefcase and laptop computer. Her voice mail came on, he hung up without leaving a message. Calling off an engagement wasn't the sort of thing one did over the phone.

And though he knew his plate was really full right now, he left the estate and headed back to the beach house.

None of it mattered without Whitney.

WHITNEY HEARD the whine of the automatic garage door, felt the vibration of sound as the Porsche's engine revved then shut off.

Her foot paused on the pedal of the sewing machine. Volumes of white satin and lace surrounded her, draped over her lap, spilling onto the pineapple-and celery-hued patterned rug beneath her chair. Her heart drummed and her fingers trembled. She had an urge to grab the dress, to dart into the bedroom, to hide.

Dylan came into the room through the garage door. He halted, his arms laden with bags. Her gaze met his for only an instant before it skittered away.

She sucked in a breath, pressed down on the pedal. The sewing machine whirred as she fed a seam beneath the needle.

"You're designing wedding gowns now?" he asked, his voice deep and very soft.

"No." She cleared her throat. "This is Cori's."

Silence. Either he *couldn't* speak for the moment or he merely chose not to. The tension in the room felt thick and awkward.

A gull screeched, its cry echoing through the open sliding-glass door. The surf rushed onto the sand, ebbed back to sea.

Whitney could feel his stillness even though she wasn't looking at him. She'd hoped to get this done—or at least part of it done—before he got back from the store. After all, it was a rush job and she couldn't put it off much longer.

Then again, maybe she'd subconsciously wanted to see his reaction to the dress.

His reaction to the mother of his child sewing his bride's dress.

She gathered satin from her lap, looped it over her arm and out of the way. "You probably ought to leave the room. It's bad luck for the groom to see the dress." She felt mean wishing for the superstition to come true.

And her heart stung when he *did* leave the room without another word or glance.

Chapter Ten

The smell of charcoal roused her from the alterations. A glance at her watch showed she'd been at it for over an hour. Her back ached and her muscles were protesting.

Probably from that game of volleyball. Her inner arms were a bit swollen and faintly bruised from smacking the ball.

She shut off the sewing machine, hung the wedding dress back on its padded hanger and zipped it into a plastic bag. Just a couple more tucks and it would be finished. Hopefully. No telling how good the fit would be since Cori hadn't bothered to remove her clothes.

Oh, well. Frankly, Whitney didn't want to think about Cori or the dress or the upcoming wedding. Dylan was on her patio preparing a barbecue.

For the two of them.

For five days, he was still hers.

And though that gave her a punch of guilt, made her feel just a little mean-spirited, she dismissed it. The time for sacrificing would come soon enough. Until then, she would enjoy him.

She slid open the screen door, stepped onto the

wood deck. He'd changed into jeans and a gray T-shirt. High-top tennis shoes, looking old and well-worn, were on his feet, the laces undone and dragging the ground.

She smiled. "You're going to break your neck if you take a step." His boyish grin as he glanced over his shoulder made her stomach cartwheel.

"Didn't your Paris trip teach you anything about men's style?"

"Grunge for a guy your age isn't in."

"Ouch. I could have done without that age remark."

She patted his shoulder. "Muscles talking to you after that game?"

"Nope. My muscles are just fine, thanks. How about yours?"

"I can be big and admit that mine are smarting a bit."

His brow furrowed, and concern flashed across his features. "Looks like it's time to make good on those massages I owe you."

He started to reach for her. She ducked, went to stand by the wood railing, looked out at the ocean.

"No...uh, no, I'm fine, really. It's only a twinge. It'll straighten out in the Jacuzzi tub." There was no way those hands of his were getting that close to her body. Regardless of his tally, massages were definitely out. The rules of their game had changed.

"So, why wait for a bath when I've got a perfectly good set of willing hands right here?" He held up those perfectly good hands and Whitney's heart did a few more acrobatics. If it didn't settle down, that was going to be another sore muscle to add to the list.

She had to think fast. "The sun's about to set. If you start massaging me, I'll turn to a puddle and miss the whole thing."

She shivered in the breeze, rubbed at her arms, then sat on the padded chaise longue, her gaze trained on the ball of fire about to sink below the horizon. The sea burst with color, like flames licking off the surface, while the sky blazed in a glorious pallet so vivid it made her breathless.

She felt warmth surround her and glanced up as Dylan draped a chenille afghan around her shoulders. "Thanks."

"Sure thing. Want a beer while we wait for these coals to get hot?" He stopped, shook his head. "No, you need milk."

That drew her attention right away from nature's spectacular show. She sent him a ferocious look. "Don't be cute."

"I'm not being cute. Well, I *am* cute, but…"

She whacked him on the arm.

"Ouch. What was that for?"

"You sounded like a stuck record. I was getting you *un*stuck." She tugged him down into the lounge chair beside hers. "Forget the predinner cocktails and watch the sunset. You keep carrying on and being so darn *cute* and I'm going to miss the whole thing."

He grinned and scooted his chair closer to hers, making it seem like a double lounge. His thigh brushed hers as he reached for part of the afghan.

She'd been going to mention something about him being so close. His reaching for the blanket squelched it. How could she begrudge him the warmth? Sure, it was spring, but the April nights were still quite chilly.

Shoulder to shoulder, they huddled under the blanket and watched as the last sliver of the sun sank from sight. As always, she held her breath at that final minute, the seconds where the water came alive with the molten essence of the sun, looked bloodred, as if it would boil you alive if you swam to that spot, touched it.

Her head rested on Dylan's shoulder. Somehow her hand had slipped into his. The blanket kept the chill of the wind away. The fire from the barbecue leaped and smoked, smelling of summers and family times and happiness and love. So many memories associated with a single smell.

She and Dylan had spent hours on various beaches, around fire rings or barbecue pits, always surrounded by friends, family, laughter.

Love.

She shifted, brushed her hair from her eyes. "That fire looks pretty hot to me. Want me to go get the steaks?"

"No. You just sit tight. I'm cooking."

"There's no reason why I can't help."

"I told you I'd do meals, now hush and let me do my part. Besides, you worked this afternoon and I just fooled around."

He got up and went into the kitchen through the sliding-glass door. Yes, she'd worked that afternoon. On his bride's dress.

Oh, God. The day was almost over, putting her that much closer to losing him. She wanted to stop the clock, grab those mechanical hands in her fists and hold back the inevitable.

Knowing she couldn't made her want to weep.

"YOU'RE AN EXCELLENT COOK." Sated and feeling lazy, Whitney sat on the deck, her hands wrapped around a steaming mug of cocoa. The stars were like diamonds scattered across rich ebony velvet. This stretch of beach was far enough from town where the lights didn't drown out the stars.

"Glad you liked it, madam. I'm taking requests for breakfast."

Whitney didn't pick up that particular conversational ball. Mornings were rough, and breakfast was better left for brunch. She looked away, saw Brett on his patio next door.

He waved and she waved back.

Dylan made a groaning noise in the back of his throat.

"What?"

"Do you have to encourage Blondie that way?"

"What do you mean, encourage? I just waved at him. He's my neighbor."

"Yeah, well now he's coming over here."

She inhaled the sweet aroma of chocolate, hiding her smile. Dylan Montgomery was pea green jealous.

It tickled her.

Brett jogged the short distance across the sand, mounted the steps to her patio.

"How's it going, you two?"

"Fine," Dylan answered before Whitney could even get her mouth open. He was annoyed that the other man had intruded on their peace. They had stars overhead, a romantic, rhythmic surf, the smell of the sea and rich sweet chocolate.

This was the time of day when a couple could

unwind, talk about the day, make plans for the next. That's what he'd been trying to do before Whitney's grinning neighbor had butted in.

"I came to ask about the festival. You interested in going this week?"

Brett's eyes were on Whitney, the question directed at her.

"I've got sewing to do..."

Exactly, Dylan thought. *Some* of us have to work. Well, technically he was on a sort of vacation, but shouldn't blond guy here have to go off to a job or something. Or was he just a rich beach bum?

"I'll be tied up at the office the next couple of days, but I thought we could walk over there Wednesday evening."

Oh, so Coleman *did* work. And if Dylan didn't pay attention here, he was going to be left home to twiddle his thumbs.

He put his arm around Whitney's shoulders, surprising her into silence when he pressed his lips fleetingly to her temple. "We're free that night, aren't we, Slim? And you know how you love to listen to jazz."

Brett's sandy-blond brows drew together and his laser-sharp gaze rested on Dylan for just an instant. Annoyed.

Good.

Then, good humor restored, Brett grinned. "Great. Seven o'clock all right with you?"

"Yep," Dylan said. "Sounds good. Bring a date, why don't you?"

By this time, Whitney was pinching his thigh beneath the blanket, and pulling the short hairs on his leg—and all the while smiling sweetly. "Thanks for asking, Brett. *I'm* looking forward to it."

Brett winked. "Okay, see you guys Wednesday." He went down the stairs and jogged back across the sand.

Whitney turned to look at Dylan. He was already looking at her. Their noses bumped. He smelled wonderful. His eyes shone with those devilish lights.

She could not be annoyed with him if she tried.

Instead, she laughed. "You are bad."

"So. You don't really go for his type. I know you."

"Says who?"

"Says me."

"So what is my type?" Too late. She knew it even before the words left her mouth.

"Me." His lips closed over hers.

Like chocolate left in the warm sun, she melted into the kiss, naturally, immediately, no questions asked or protests given. She wanted it, ached for it.

He was so warm, so familiar. His essence wrapped around her, drew her in. He pulled her closer until her breasts nestled against his side, their soft weight giving against his firm chest. Desire flashed, swift and incendiary, whipping her into a frenzy of need before she could even take a breath.

She wanted to rush, to horde, to grab every moment she had with him, close it in her fist, go back for more, to not waste a millisecond of time or miss a single taste or memory.

His tongue enticed and soothed. His hands framed her face, angled her head. For an instant he pulled back, gazed at her, his brown eyes intense, asking questions she had no answers for.

"Kiss me," she whispered. "Just for a while. Just a little."

It was wrong. But it felt right.

Dylan didn't have to be asked twice. He was where he wanted to be—with Whitney in his arms, her hands on his shoulders, her scent surrounding him, her textures teasing and sating him.

This is what life could be, *should* be. They'd played together, talked together, flirted with one another, laughed and reacted. It was easy. And it was fun. And it was right.

This is how it would be with Whitney permanently in his world, day in and day out, morning and night and all the in-betweens, from now until forever.

Perfect.

He loved the taste of her, the feel, that little sound she made in the back of her throat, the way her knee bounced, even now, the way she put herself whole-heartedly into everything she did.

She gave so unselfishly. And he wanted to take. But he wanted to give, too.

He felt the beat of her heart against his chest, knew it matched his own. He could easily lift her in his arms, carry her into the bedroom with its lemon walls and rainbow-sherbet accents and scent of white gardenias. She would go with him now.

But instinctively, he knew the timing wasn't right. Last night she'd had the terrible headache. Today, there had been revelations, and a whole scale of ups and downs.

He wanted more time to just *be* with her before he pushed. He wanted to make darn sure he didn't blow it.

Because if he made a mistake, lost Whitney now,

he wouldn't be able to face the tough decisions that needed to be made by the end of the week.

She must have sensed his indecision, his turmoil. She eased out of the kiss, rested her forehead against his, then scooted back and looked at him.

"Well, if I'd known what a great kisser you were, I'd have suggested we do more of it years ago."

"Likewise." It surprised him that he could even speak. "I don't know where my mind was back then."

She straightened her clothes, flicked her hair behind her ears. "On Brittany Sommers or Tammy Wainright or Linda Verdes or—"

"Okay, okay. I was an idiot."

She smothered a laugh. "You said it, I didn't."

He grinned, pleased to note that her hands were trembling, that her knee was bouncing faster and faster. "Well, you were pretty tied up most of the time, too."

"Not like you. I was into school activities."

"Yeah, like the star quarterback?"

"I only dated him for a week."

"Because that lanky basketball player—what's his name?"

"Wes."

"Yeah, Wes the Wuss snagged your eye." He put a hand on her bouncing knee.

"He wasn't a wuss."

"Just a two-timer."

"Exactly."

His brows shot up. "I swear you'd argue with a signpost."

"I'm not arguing, I'm just making sure we get our name-calling correct—he wasn't a wuss, but he *was* a two-timer.'' Whitney made herself scoot a little farther away, prepare to stand. It was very hard to do. ''And I'm surprised you remember the names of my high school sweethearts so well.''

''I imagine a lot of the things I remember would surprise you. In fact, recently, they're surprising *me*.''

Oh, dear, they were about to get off on subjects better left untouched. She'd agreed to let him stay the week. As friends. That kiss was taking things way beyond friendship.

And though they'd already gone way beyond friendship, there was no sense compounding the error. No sense in adding more bittersweet memories to haunt her in the dead of night—or her every waking hour.

She stood at last and reached for his empty cocoa mug, feeling cold to the bone without his body heat to warm her.

''I think I'll turn in now. Uh, the bed in the guest room has clean sheets. If you need another blanket, it's in the hall closet.'' And so was the wedding dress. Where in the world was she going to put that darn thing?

''I know where everything is. I'll be in later.''

She turned, went through the sliding-glass door. Those same four words had surely been uttered countless times, by countless couples. Married couples.

But she and Dylan weren't married.

Would never be married.

Because he was promised to somebody else.

THE SUN STREAMED IN the bedroom window, competing with the lemon walls and soft pastel fabrics, casting happiness all around the room.

Whitney's stomach didn't feel happy at all.

Kicking the covers, she wrestled her way out of the bed. Her foot connected with the nightstand, sending the alarm clock and a silver-framed photograph crashing against the wall, bouncing to the floor.

She didn't try to catch either item, never even thought to avert disaster. Her only mission was to make it to the bathroom.

The door crashed back on its hinge. She dropped to her knees on the buttery rug, wanted to die, wished for it, prayed for it.

She didn't hear her bedroom door open, didn't hear the footsteps. All she heard was the buzzing in her ears, the blood pounding at her temples, the litany in her mind... *Oh, please, oh, please, oh, please. It hurts. I don't feel good. I don't want to do this.*

A gentle hand at her head startled her. Strong fingers stroked, gathered her hair away from her face. He knelt beside her.

Now she *really* wanted to die. She was mortified beyond belief, tried to wave him away. When that didn't work, she gave a push.

She was weak as a kitten. That's the only excuse she could come up with for why he didn't budge. At any other time, she could have sent him sprawling across the floor.

"Shh, don't fight me."

Tears spilled over her lids, dampened her cheeks. She wasn't crying, she told herself. She wasn't feeling sorry for herself. Her eyes were just watering from the indelicate, stomach-wrenching bout of morning sickness.

"Go away," she finally managed to rasp.

A cool washcloth wiped across the back of her neck, over her cheeks. "Not on a bet, Slim."

She reached up, flushed the toilet, pulled her knees up to her chest and rested her head on them. She wasn't sure it was wise to move just now.

"Okay?" he asked softly.

"Don't talk to me…please," she added, trying not to sound mean. But if she had to talk, she'd surely be sick again. She just needed to be still, to be quiet. It would pass.

He stroked her hair, her back, soothing her, respecting her request for silence. Chills raced over her arms, dotted her legs as cool air hit her clammy skin.

Knowing she couldn't sit on the bathroom floor all day with Dylan staring at her as if she were about to expire right before his eyes, she stood, rinsed her mouth, and splashed more water on her face.

With her palms braced against the sink, she hung her head. Lord, these episodes took all the stuffing out of her. Her legs trembled and sweat trickled between her breasts.

What an absolutely horrible way to start such a sunny morning.

Dylan couldn't stand seeing the pale, miserable look on her face. She was a strong, capable, sassy woman, but right now, all it would take was a little bitty gust of wind to knock her flat. And that made his heart ache, made his gut clench.

He reached down, hooked his arm under her knees and lifted her. When she started to protest, he gave her a fierce look.

"Just shut up, Slim." God, he'd take this part of it on himself if it were possible. And for a minute there, he almost thought it *was* possible. He was feeling a little queasy himself.

She didn't fight him or take him to task for telling her to shut up. Instead she dropped her head to his shoulder, curled into him with utter trust.

A lump formed in his throat. He eased her onto the mattress, smoothed her hair off her forehead, pressed his lips to her brow.

"Does this happen every morning?"

"Mostly."

"How long will it last?"

She shrugged. "I looked it up in a book. It could last days or the whole nine months. And it doesn't always confine itself to mornings."

"Oh, man."

He looked absolutely stricken in a way that only a man could, and Whitney found the energy to smile. "So far, I've been lucky, and it passes pretty quick. Tea helps—provided I can make it to the kitchen to brew it."

He jumped up, jolting the mattress, and Whitney waited to determine whether her stomach was going to revolt again.

"You stay put. I'll go get it."

She watched him rush out of the room. Lord, she didn't want to depend on him, to get used to this. She only had him for the week. Then she'd be on her own again, back to crawling to the kitchen, or just curling into a fetal position until the horrible sickness passed.

She gently pressed a hand to her stomach. How

could something so precious—such a beautiful miracle—wreak this much havoc?

DYLAN FINISHED CLEANING the kitchen. He hadn't been able to talk Whitney into eating anything more substantial than tea and soda crackers until almost noon. Certain that wasn't enough nourishment for a woman growing a baby in her womb—*his* baby— he'd finally tempted her with fresh fruit and French toast made with thick slices of whole grain bread he'd picked up at the farmer's market in town.

Whitney Emerson had never met a piece of French toast she could refuse, and he'd used that knowledge to his advantage.

He'd felt proud of himself, personally responsible when the color had returned to her cheeks. After all, he was the one who'd gotten her in this fix to begin with. Technically it was his fault that she was so ill.

A baby.

With the turmoil of the wedding, and the mess of the company, and the gut-slamming emotions that had hit him like the fire of torpedoes when he'd seen Whitney again, learned her secret, he hadn't truly given a lot of thought to the baby. It hadn't felt real. He hadn't really pictured it.

Now he did. In his mind's eye he could see Whitney growing round, still active, her skin glowing, her hand resting on her tummy, love shining in her eyes. He could see her holding a tiny child, a child who carried both their genes.

Dylan wasn't conceited, but he knew he was a better than average-looking guy. And Whitney was a knockout. Together they would produce beautiful children.

A boy or a girl? he wondered. Whichever, he didn't care. Funny that just as he'd never really considered marriage, he'd also never really thought about children. At thirty-two, the thought should have crossed his mind.

An echo of his father's words rang in his subconscious. *You'll do as I did—settle down and marry at thirty-two.* Those word had been uttered not long before the fatal heart attack. Had Randolph even then meddled and pushed, knowing Dylan's fascination with laser technology, arranged the merger offer? Planted the marriage idea between him and Cori Spencer?

At the time, Dylan had let his father's arrogant words and hearty slap on the back go in one ear and out the other. He'd learned the best way to keep peace was to simply nod as though he agreed, then go on about his own business. Had he perhaps done that when Randolph had mentioned this cruise ship stabilizer venture? The defunct venture that was now threatening everything he held dear in his life?

Ah, hell. He didn't have any of the answers.

Wiping his damp palms on his jeans, he made his way out of the kitchen in search of Whitney. The lingering smell of maple syrup vied with the briny scent of the ocean breeze wafting through the sliding-glass doors.

He glanced around at the sunny interior of the beach house. Karl had let Whitney decorate it, and true to her sense of fun and style, she'd chosen colors and prints that were a feast for the eyes—lemon and pineapple yellows, mango oranges, misty seafoam greens. The colors alone should have made him feel hungry. Instead they made him feel peaceful, happy, safe.

The floors were glossy cream tiles covered with patterned rugs. The art on the walls was an eclectic blend of whimsical and classic—a blue dog with a startled look in his wide yellow eyes, a bowl of tangerines spilling out onto a mantel, a field of flowers and ladybugs. Every piece of art, furniture or color made a person want to smile.

And when he saw Whitney, he realized that she, too, made a person just want to smile.

She had a pin cushion strapped to her wrist but half the straight pins were sticking out of her mouth. She wore a pair of jeans that hugged low on her hips and belled out at the calf, the frayed hems dragging the ground. Her feet were bare, her toes painted a delicate pink. Three slim gold rings decorated her middle toe. Her lavender tank top had spaghetti straps, rode *really* low over the swell of her breasts, and barely reached the waistband of her jeans, allowing her stomach to play peek-a-boo every time she lifted her arms. Her tummy had always been flat with a line of muscle definition that made women green with envy. Now it was rounded, pooching just a bit over the top of the low-slung jeans.

Pooching with his baby.

Man alive, she was sexy as all get-out.

Typically, his body reacted and he forced his gaze away to safer territory. Fabrics in an array of vivid color were piled around her, scattered over chair arms and table surfaces and spilling onto the floor. The mannequin he'd carted in yesterday was draped with some sort of sheer black fabric that sported bold splashes of orange and crimson blossoms.

Pattern pieces were all over the place, the tackle box filled with sewing apparatus was open and had been scratched through. There didn't appear to be any order to what she was doing, in fact, the room looked a bit like a mad dog had gotten loose in it. But he'd bet she could put her finger on any single item in a second if asked to.

She'd told him more than once that everyone needed a nest. This was hers, and God help anybody that messed with it until she decided to pick it up. She was in creating mode.

And she was an absolute pleasure to watch.

"Didn't anybody teach you not to play with sharp objects in your mouth?" He couldn't get over the difference in her. This morning she'd been violently ill. Now she was busy as a bee in pollen season, humming to herself—off-key—radiating an aura of energy that made him feel tired just watching.

She looked up, distracted. In her creative mode, he thought again.

Then her brow cleared and her smile came with it as she removed the pins from between her lips and set them aside. "Nope, just the opposite. Uncle Karl said always be prepared to take a nip or tuck here or there, to pin up a makeshift idea before you forget it."

"I don't recall seeing him with pins in his mouth."

"That's because he's got more couth than I do." She walked toward him, her gaze going from the unfolded bolt of fabric in her hands, to his face, then back again.

"Here, let me see what this color of orange does to your skintone."

Before he could duck, she'd draped him in expensive cashmere. "What?"

"Hush." She tucked an end under his arm from behind, swagged it across his front like a cowl, then flipped it over his other shoulder, making sure it tucked right up next to his chin. "Not bad."

The way her gaze touched on the fabric, then on his eyes, made him go hot. "Not bad? Somebody ought to be shot for dying cashmere this color."

"It's a stylish color. It'll sell."

He was skeptical. "At least it's soft. What are you going to do with it?"

"A form-fitting skirt with a slit up to here." She pointed to a spot high on her thigh. "A little twin set camisole and cardigan—hip-length, I think. Stay right there."

She grabbed his hands, had him hold the bolt of pumpkin-colored cashmere right where she'd put it— draped around his neck like a whisper-soft kitten— then dashed across the room and unearthed two more cardboard bolts thickly wrapped with fabric.

Next she pinned a swathe of black satin around his hips like a floor-length slip, then draped him in a second layer, using an equal measure of that sheer black tulle stuff that sported gaudy flowers, and pinned it all in place.

She accomplished the design task so quickly he barely had time to formulate a thought, to find just the right words to object. Crazily, it reminded him of a pit stop in an Indy 500 race—zip in, jack it up, tires off, tires on, slam it down, go.

He finally gained his vocal cords, tried to take a step. "Whitney..."

"Hold still or you'll get stuck."

She sank to her knees. Right there in front of him.
Oh, man.

His brain supplied plenty of suggestive pictures.
His body needed little encouragement to react, never
mind that he was draped in a skirt, being used as a
human mannequin—female at that.

Whitney pinned a cuff for a hem, gave a tug,
looked up.

And nearly fainted at the blast of heat shining out
of Dylan's brown eyes.

Chapter Eleven

For the life of her, Whitney couldn't look away from the intense heat in Dylan's gaze. He should have looked silly—feminine even—standing there draped in pumpkin cashmere and diaphanous black silk.

He'd never looked more virile in his life.

His hands closed around her upper arms and she found herself standing, pressed against the front of him. Double-faced cashmere teased her belly where her tank top had ridden up. She stared at his brown eyes, his sculpted, unsmiling mouth, the creases in his forehead that told her his thoughts were deep.

Soul deep.

His head started to lower, excruciatingly slow. His eyes remained on hers. She was afraid to move. Afraid not to.

Outside the surf ebbed and flowed, gulls wheeled and screeched, palm fronds rustled in the breeze. The smell of suntan oil wafted through the open windows as one of her neighbors no doubt prepared to bask in the spring sunshine.

She could see the pores in Dylan's skin, the white squint lines textured by the sun, the minute ebony starbursts fanning the pupils of his deep brown eyes.

His breath brushed her cheek, her lips, smelling of syrup and melon and man. And still her gaze was drawn back to those eyes, eyes she could fall into, eyes aflame with desire and intent, the intent of a man who'd set his sights on a woman. On her.

The thrill that shot through her nearly made her sag to the floor. His hold on her arms kept her on her feet. She'd never seen such a look on Dylan's face, never expected to in all the years they'd been buddies.

Oh, she'd hoped. And that night three months ago, they'd come close.

But still, it was nothing like right now.

The heat nearly scorched her.

And it scared her silly.

Putting an end to the torture, she came to her senses, jerked back, severing the moment like the swift snip of razor-sharp scissors.

The corners of his mouth tipped up in the barest hint of a smile. He knew he affected her. He knew he could have her. He knew she wanted him to have her.

But he wouldn't push or coerce. He was going to drive her nuts with his patience. Make her think about it. Picture it. Worry over it. Anticipate it. Reach for it.

Oh, for Pete's sake!

She took a breath, slid the straight pins out of the fabric draping his waist, her fingers trembling. He made her lose all sense of time and place, made her forget what was at stake between them.

A wedding dress hanging in her bedroom closet was a really good reminder and she tried to focus on that.

His hand covered hers. "You better let me do that."

Oh, Lord, his voice was deep and rich and aroused. He might look at her with amused indulgence at her evading tactics, but he was certainly not unaffected. It was nearly her undoing.

She stepped back, carefully rolled the fabrics back onto their bolts as he released the pins.

She didn't dare look at the front of his jeans.

She heard him moving around behind her, heard him suck in a breath.

"I think I'll go for a jog, maybe take a swim. Want to join me?"

As much as she could use a sobering splash of icy water, she knew better. She needed to keep as many clothes on as possible.

"No, thanks, you go ahead. I've got some more work to do." She started to mention the wedding dress, just to put up some much needed barriers between them, but for some reason couldn't bring herself to do it.

She glanced over her shoulder, gave him a smile, wondered if her facial muscles were jumping and trembling like her insides. "Thanks for modeling for me."

He winked. "Anytime, Slim."

WHITNEY MADE an honest attempt to shimmy into a clean pair of jeans—her favorite ones—dancing around the room, trying to get them zipped. Something drastic and awful had happened to her figure somewhere between the weekend and today.

Had a measly plate of French toast done this much damage?

She considered lying on the bed to get the pants fastened, but dismissed it, staring in disgust at her reflection in the mirror. With her sewing obligations, she *had* been sitting on her butt a lot lately, but surely that hadn't caused her hips to spread out to this extent. Had the denim shrunk in a too hot dryer?

It was too early for the pregnancy to do this... wasn't it? And surely it didn't just all of a sudden happen over night. She was fairly certain she'd worn these same jeans just a couple of days ago.

She turned sideways, ran her hand over her abdomen. A definite pooch, a firm knot right here under the smooth skin. Her insides fluttered, tickled, and her heart danced.

A baby. A sweet-faced cherub with tiny dimples and velvet-brown eyes. A little bitty replica of Dylan.

She focused her attention back on the full-length mirror and nearly cursed. There she stood with acid-washed denim sucked to her thighs like shrink-wrap and hanging open in a wide vee in the front without a prayer of zipping.

And even if she *could* get the zipper up, she'd be miserable, probably choke her poor baby in the process.

Peeling the jeans back down her legs was another fiasco and she was sweating and irritable by the time she completed the chore.

"Slim?" Dylan called from the hallway. "You about ready?"

"Five minutes." *Right*. She hurled the jeans toward the closed door and they landed with a plop over the top of the waste can. Fine. After that nasty experience they deserved to be thrown away.

Opting for comfort this time, she stepped into a

pair of white cotton overalls that were a full two sizes
too large—at least they *had* been—then added a
fluffy pink, torso-hugging, cropped mohair sweater
for both fun and warmth, and hooked the metal tabs
over her shoulders. A pair of shiny pink patent
leather high-topped tennis shoes rounded out the ensemble.

A dash of gloss on her lips, a pinch to her cheeks
and a couple more clips in her messy up-do hairstyle
and she was ready to go. And not much over her five
minutes, either. She wasn't one to be coy, to make
an entrance. She believed in being on time, and it
was very close to the time when Brett had agreed to
meet them to walk over to the festival.

Dylan looked up when Whitney breezed into the
room, and he went very, very still, both inside and
out. She could make a pair of farmer's overalls look
like high fashion and cause a man to forget every
intelligent thought in his head.

Her hair was swept up with a few sexy, dark tendrils falling around her face, making him ache to
press his lips to the back of her neck....

"Is something wrong?" She fussed with the metal
tabs that hooked straps to the bib—right close to the
upper swell of her breasts.

"Nothing wrong. You look cute."

She grinned, did a little spin. "I was aiming for
funky, but cute will do."

"How about good enough to eat?"

That caused her to pause midspin. She opened her
mouth but no words came out.

He took a step closer. "You're thinking about it,
aren't you, Slim?"

She caught his double meaning and her cheeks

pinked, turning a much darker shade than her fuzzy
top. With a knack for bad timing, Brett Coleman interrupted the moment by knocking on the back door.
"Hey, anybody home?"

Dylan held her gaze for a few seconds more, deliberately ignoring their visitor—who, by the way,
could see right through the open sliding-glass door
that they were indeed home.

Whitney cleared her throat, her gaze darting to the
door. She lifted her hand to flick her hair behind her
ear, realized it was up in a clip and dropped her arm,
lacing her fingers together instead.

Everything on her and in her was shaking, right
down to her bones. Yes, she was definitely thinking
about *it*.

And Dylan was giving her a hungry look that
made her want to yank the drapes closed and slam
the door on Brett Coleman and his perky blond side-
kick.

She did neither. Instead she pasted a smile on her
face, made a wide skirting path around Dylan and
moved toward their guests.

"Come on in, Brett. We're ready to go." She
looked at the blonde, the designer in her automatically assessing the powder-blue polyester pants and
trendy jacket with its huge, fabric-covered buttons.
Nice, she thought. A black backpack purse rode the
balls of her shoulders, and slip-on clogs decorated
her feet. And decoration was the optimal word. They
weren't walking shoes. In fashion, yes, but imprac-
tical for where they were going. "Hi, Sally. Glad you
could join us."

Sally smiled. "I got the feeling Brett needed a
strong shoulder."

Because Whitney had chosen to be with Dylan when clearly Brett had wanted to date her. The reference made Whitney wince.

But Brett took it in good stride, grinning his congenial grin, the one that invited everybody to be friends. He put his hands on Sally's shoulders, gave a squeeze. "And you have such nice shoulders, Sal."

Whitney saw the change in the other woman, the barely discernible indrawn breath, the slight lift of her chest, the heightened color. Beach Babe Sally had a thing for Brett. And judging by the fleeting frown, the distracted glance, Brett was just now noticing it. "Okay, let's go."

They walked the two blocks to the center of town, to the main street that flowed onto the pier. The street had been closed off for the festival and only pedestrian traffic was allowed. Along the sidewalks, surf shops and coffeehouses kept their doors open way past closing hours, racking up additional sales. Stalls selling T-shirts, trinkets, crafts and local art lined the center of the street. There were also carnival fun booths with shelves crammed with stuffed animals to be won by tossing rings or shooting tin ducks that marched in a row.

Opportunities for a friendly round of competition were plentiful, and Whitney eyed them all with consideration.

"Name your poison," Dylan said close to her ear. He could see her desire to play.

His own desire was to touch. That sweater was soft, invited a man's hands to stroke and caress. And so did her skin. She glowed with good health and he was really happy about that. Especially after her earlier comment about this baby sickness stuff hitting at all hours of the day.

Thank God she was only having it in the mornings. So far.

Brett and Sally had walked on ahead and disappeared into the crowd. Just as well. They didn't make a good foursome anyway. And Dylan wasn't in the mood to share Whitney's attention.

"Care for a shooting match?" Whitney asked.

He tsked, shook his head. "The woman never learns. What're the stakes? Or am I giving you a handicap this time?"

She punched him on the arm. "The day you have to give me a handicap is the day I'm lying dead over in Dillard's cemetery." She reached in her pocket for money, glared at Dylan when he gently elbowed her aside and paid for the both of them to have a turn at picking off ducks.

She lifted the air gun to her shoulder, sighted, studied her targets, gave an experimental pull of the trigger. The sight was low and to the left. She compensated for that and knocked every one of those cute little ducks down, drawing a small crowd as the pings sounded one right after the other.

"Deadeye," Dylan commented.

"Close." She snatched out more money from her pocket and slapped it on the wooden ledge. "Once more."

This time she knew where to aim, and again the pings rang in quick succession. She hit every one of the targets. Rather than bells ringing, there was a cacophony of quacking.

She lowered the gun, laughed at the silliness of it all, and pointed to the animal she wanted—a soft black puppy that sprawled with all four legs aiming in different directions.

It was Dylan's turn to shoot. He raised his gun, squinted, pulled the trigger twice quickly, missed, paused, then getting the sight correct, knocked over the rest of his targets until his gun ran out of ammo.

Whitney paid for another round for him, too. "That was just practice. Now redeem yourself."

He did, but Whitney had already won the competition. Because on his first turn he'd missed two ducks and she'd only missed one.

He was a good sport about it, though. He had to be. They'd done this too many times in the past. Sometimes he won, and sometimes she did. No matter, they always had fun.

The booth worker asked which animal Dylan wanted. He looked at Whitney. "Well, Slim. Take another pick."

"Nope. It was your win. You choose."

"I'd choose you," he said softly.

She gave his arm a shake as though there truly was nothing more between them than friendship. The whitening of the scar over her lip told a different story. "The toys, silly."

"Fine. I'll take that white cat up there." When the guy handed it to him, he tried to pass it to Whitney.

"Why should I carry it? You won and picked it. It's yours."

"You should hold it for your own protection."

"How do you figure that?"

"Because looking at that fuzzy sweater is giving me lots of ideas. Every time you move or breath, I want to reach over and touch, to pet."

"Oh."

Her cheeks pinked again, and Dylan was charmed. He'd never known Whitney Emerson to blush so often, and so prettily. It was obvious that she was flustered, was having trouble pretending indifference, keeping up the act.

Good.

He chuckled when she hugged the stuffed cat to her chest, eyed him as though he were about to pounce. Then she seemed to realize what she was doing, and she laughed. Twirling, she handed both fluffy toys to a little girl with crooked pigtails and a missing front tooth.

Whitney was glad to have her hands free. She was a toucher by nature, and wanted both hands available in case she came upon a fine texture, or in case she lost her mind and had to touch Dylan.

Which she did, unconsciously, when she saw a cotton candy vendor.

With her hand on his arm, she pointed. "I haven't had cotton candy in ages. Let's get some." They only had two full days left to be together like this and she was determined to make the very most of them.

"Before dinner?"

Whitney rolled her eyes. "You sound like a fussy mother. Of course we can have it before dinner. We can have it *instead* of dinner if we like. After all, we're both well over twenty-one and haven't had anybody impose rules for a long time."

"I'm glad you've brought that up. And I'm glad you've had a change of heart."

"What change of heart?"

"About imposing rules."

She frowned. "What does that have to do with cotton candy?"

"Nothing."

"Then you've lost me."

"Rules, Slim. You've been imposing them lately and I aim to break them."

She had a funny feeling about this. "Which ones?"

"The one where you've said we can't be lovers."

She blinked, swallowed hard. "Did I actually say that?"

"Yes."

"Well, it's a good rule. Appropriate."

He shook his head. "It's a lousy rule. And I can't go by it."

"We're—"

He put his fingers over her mouth, cutting off the words he knew she was about to say. "Friends, yes. But I'm saying we can't *just* be friends anymore."

"Well, we can't be lovers, either." Frantically she looked around for Brett and Sally. She needed a buffer. The other couple had gone their own way, were nowhere in sight.

"Says who?"

"Says me…"

"Over twenty-one, remember? No rules. And all this talking about it is just making me want you more."

"It's not just my rule, Dylan. You're getting married Saturday!"

A muscle ticked at his jaw. Suddenly he went very still, then he burst into action, cupping her cheeks— surprisingly gentle for the fierce look on his face, for the emotions emanating from him—and in front of half the town and a good many tourists, to boot, Dylan Montgomery kissed her as if the world were about to end and this was his last desperate chance.

For endless seconds she didn't move, didn't respond, *couldn't* respond. The power of the kiss whipped through her, blanking her mind, stunning her with its force. And when she finally caught up with the strange delay of her body and mind, when she finally raised up on tiptoe to lean into the kiss, to savor, to participate, to enjoy and take and give, it was over.

She darn near fell face-first when he stepped back. Only his firm hold on her arms prevented it. She stared at him, her lips throbbing, her heart pounding, her cheeks flaming. She was way too hot under this furry sweater.

Not sure if her vocal cords would work, she cleared her throat. "What...what was that for?"

"You have to ask?"

She glanced away. There was no denying that the chemistry between them was very powerful. Lust, she told herself, was a very powerful thing.

And that's what Dylan felt. Surely that's all he felt.

She took a steadying breath, hooked her arm through his, tortured herself with the feel of his warm body next to hers, the strength of his muscled arm resting against the side of her sensitized breast.

"All this over cotton candy. Sometimes you make me crazy, Dylan Montgomery." Rather than stop at the candy booth, she steered him to an open-air fish counter along the wooden pier. "I'll compromise here and buy you a bowl of this world famous clam chowder."

"Every food vendor on this pier is advertising theirs as world famous. Which one do we believe?"

"Hmm." She stopped smack in the middle of the pier, nearly causing a pedestrian pile-up.

Dylan slipped his arm around her waist, pulled her out of harm's way. She never even noticed the baby stroller that was about to clip her heels.

"That guy over there looks pretty honest to me," she said. "Suppose his is the authentic stuff?"

Dylan joined the game. "I don't know. He's got green eyes. That could spell trouble."

"*I've* got green eyes," she objected.

"Yep. And you're definitely trouble."

"Do you want clam chowder or not? If you don't, just say so and we'll go with my first plan and get the candy."

"I didn't say I didn't want it. But we want to make sure it's the best."

Her breath hissed in mock aggravation. "Okay, smarty, which one is the best?"

"That one." He pointed to a woman wearing way too few clothes, especially for a night that held a biting chill. Once the sun set over the ocean, it might as well have been the dead of winter the way the breeze cut right through a person. Even now, Whitney was shivering slightly and she was wearing a furry sweater.

"Figures," she said, jabbing an elbow in his ribs. "You just like what's under that skimpy T-shirt."

"She's got something under her T-shirt?"

Whitney dragged him over to the original vendor. "You're just asking to be pushed off this pier, buddy."

"And you'd go right down with me."

She laughed, loving the way they could tease one another. And he was right. Dylan was no gentleman when it came to competitiveness between them. If she was crazily inclined to knock him off this old wooden pier into the dark waters of the Pacific, she'd better be prepared to take an evening swim, too. She and Dylan were a team, did things as one.... She slammed her mind on the torturous realization that very soon that would no longer be the case.

The sourdough bread bowls were filled with rich, creamy chowder swimming with plump clams. The heat warmed her hands and her insides, the aroma vying with the heavy smell of creosote from the wooden planks of the pier as well as the fishy smell of the harbor and the sugary scents of candy.

Whitney finished the soup then fought the foolish lump in her throat when Dylan bought her a huge, fluffy cone of pink spun sugar.

It was sticky and wonderful, tapping into myriad memories, memories that she shared with Dylan. This festival was held every year, had been for as long as she could remember. And every year, they'd come together.

Of course this time was different. This time when they walked, they touched in a different way. This time when they looked, they gazed in a different way. And this time when they danced to the bluesy strains of the jazz band, they moved in a different way.

A fine hum of desperation colored their every look or action. Whitney could feel it, and it made her ache. The clock was ticking. This would be their last pier festival together...at least, this way.

So she hoarded the sensations, eased closer into

his arms, felt the heat of his chest, the beat of his heart, felt the bittersweet love in her own heart swell as tears stung the backs of her closed eyelids.

She wanted this night to go on forever. Knew that it couldn't.

Dylan held his hand low on her back, just above the swell of her hips. Her hand rested in his palm and he pulled her close, holding their clasped fists against his heart. More strands of silky hair had come loose from her topknot and Dylan longed to scatter those pins, to run his fingers through her hair. He rested his chin on her head instead, rubbed his thumb back and forth over the incredibly soft fur of her top.

All evening she'd been tempting him with a look, a scent, a challenge. If she moved just so, and if he glanced just so, he could see right down her overalls to the smooth skin of her belly, her hips, her thighs, the rounded globes of her rear.

He fantasized about putting his hands inside those pants, of caressing, of driving her wild.

The very thought was driving *him* wild.

She flowed against him, not speaking. For that matter, he didn't feel like breaking the silence between them, either, content to just touch, feel, move, listen to the sound of the surf and the plaintive wail of the saxophone.

He felt her shiver. "Cold?"

"I'm fine."

Her warm breath fanned against his neck. Keeping her hand in his, their fingers entwined, he used his thumb to lift her chin, to bring her gaze to his.

For endless moments time seemed to stand still. Desire palpitated in deep intangible waves, mesmerizing, spinning a web, holding them in a spell.

It was the most natural thing in the world to lower his head, to touch his lips to hers, to feel the slick gloss of her lips sliding gently, erotically, against his, to taste the cotton candy on her tongue, to melt into her.

To fall in love.

Deeply in love.

She pulled back, looked at him. Something that appeared to be sadness flashed in her green eyes. He couldn't tell.

But he could tell the desire. It blazed, ruled them both.

"Not here," she whispered.

He understood. Until he could deal with his engagement, it wasn't wise to flaunt his feelings for another woman in such a public setting.

And he would deal with the engagement. Very soon.

Whitney slipped her arm around Dylan's waist and snuggled into his side as he put his arm around her shoulders. Their hips brushed and they clung as they made their way off the pier, down the streets toward the house. They'd lost track of Brett and Sally hours ago, and she didn't care. She didn't want anyone or anything to intrude on her time with Dylan.

She wished for wings so she could fly. She held tight. She knew they would make love.

He was her hope, her fantasy. Her love.

Something between them had shifted. And, yes, he was right. There were no rules. They could no longer be just friends.

Not this week anyway. For a few more days she could let down her guard, she could enjoy him, store those memories.

Just for a few more days.

Then she would revert back to the lies, the acting.

Then she would make sure Dylan did the right thing. That he saved his company, that he didn't sacrifice for her. But in the meantime, he was hers and she was going to enjoy him.

They went around the back of the house, mounted the concrete stairs from the sand. At the sliding-glass door, she stopped him, put her hand on his arm, turned her face up to his.

''No rules tonight, okay?''

Beneath the illumination of the porch light, his brown eyes went black. ''Ah, Slim...''

Her fingers pressed against his lips. ''And no promises, Dylan.''

His jaw tightened. ''What if I want those promises?''

''Then turn around and leave now.''

He stared at her for a long, humming moment. Then he shoved open the patio door, yanked her up against his chest, and backed her into the house.

Chapter Twelve

They barely made it inside the door. He flicked the metal tabs that held up her overalls, gave a tug and the oversize cotton slid right down to pool at her feet.

He never paused; he scooped her up, wrapped her legs around his hips, pressed her against the wall and kissed her with a fervor that stunned. There was nothing polite or gentle about his lips and hands.

He took.

She felt his desperation, his tremor of anger that shimmered like a hum of hot, dangerous electricity just below the surface of his skin. She wasn't sure she understood his emotions. The tension. The aggression.

She might have thought to stop the madness, afraid her heart would get broken even worse, but she was brave enough to take the chance, was powerless to do anything less than simply let him sweep her along at will. She wanted to go anywhere he might take her. Once more.

As with any challenge between them, she finally gained her senses, came out of her stupor, met his aggression, and gave it right back. Tightening her legs around his waist, she poured herself into the kiss, feasted, gave and received in return.

Her avid participation made him pause. He stepped back, his brown eyes hot, the skin still tight at the corners, his emotions still a second away from boil. "This isn't a game." His voice was unsteady, gritty.

"Then don't make it one." They were glaring at one another, chests heaving. And on fire.

It was the damnedest thing. Dylan knew he was close to losing control, but he felt like a runaway semi heading down a steep grade without an ounce of brake fluid in the lines. He was terrified, sweating, his adrenaline pumping so fast and furious he swore he could feel his bones rattle.

No promises. He wanted to shake her, force her to give him those promises.

Instead he jerked up that soft, furry top, took her breast in his mouth, pressed his hips harder into hers, wedged her tighter against the wall.

It was that little moan in the back of her throat that brought him to his senses, made him realize he was on the verge of taking her standing up against a wall, like a rutting animal.

She was the mother of his child.

He rested his forehead against hers, tried to catch his breath, almost lost it when her bare breasts rose and fell against his chest.

She was as hot as he was.

Still, that was no excuse. "I'm sorry, Slim."

"For what?"

"Treating you so rough."

She didn't want him to pull back, to come to his senses, to allow her time to come to hers. She wanted to tell him his roughness thrilled her. She'd never experienced anything like it. To have a man want her with this kind of fever was the greatest aphrodisiac, the greatest compliment—especially when that man was Dylan.

He seemed so genuinely distraught she kept her feelings to herself. It wouldn't take much for him to pull back now. And she'd die if he did.

She needed him. Just once more. She wasn't a selfish woman. But tonight—tonight she wanted to be.

With her legs still wrapped around his hips, his arousal pressing right against the core of her through lacy, French-cut panties, she wound her arms around him, held him, pressed her lips to his neck, whispered, ''Please...'' She wasn't altogether sure what she was asking for. She wanted more, wanted it all. Yet her experience was limited to their one and only time together.

And that had been so different.

Tonight her senses were sharp and vivid, awash in brilliant colors. She tasted, felt, smelled, registered everything she touched.

His kisses were like rare and unique pearls, his technique exquisitely flawless.

''Please,'' she repeated.

He watched her, silently. Still supporting her weight, he reached up, slowly removed the pins from her hair one by one, let them fall to the floor. Tendrils of hair fell in sections, tickling her cheeks, her shoulders. He drew out the process, all the while holding her gaze with his. Just that. Mesmerized. She'd never known how erotic it could be to have a man's hands in her hair, to watch the flair of his eyes as each strand came tumbling down.

At last he answered her, his voice achingly soft, sandpaper rough and deep with emotion. "Yes."

He carried her to the bedroom. She wasn't a small woman and the fact that he managed so effortlessly thrilled her. He laid her on the fluffy lemon spread, pulled the sweater the rest of the way over her head and tossed it on the floor. Then he followed her down, settled over her, cupped his hands around her scalp, threaded his fingers in her hair, held her just like that, watching her, his gaze touching her reverently, like the softest, sweetest caress.

And then he lowered his mouth to hers.

The whole experience brought a lump to her throat. She felt cherished, worshiped, like the most beautiful, desirable woman in the world.

He gave, and gave, and never expected anything in return. And she wasn't even sure she could've given anything in return if he'd asked. She was totally under his control, wrapped in a web of sensation she didn't know what to do with.

She melted into his kiss. The texture of his jeans and shirt against her bare skin was erotic. The barriers gave her fantasies wings.

There was safety there. She was vulnerable, yes, but with him fully dressed, it gave her unspoken permission to enjoy, to savor, to take her time and register each tremor, each touch and stroke and kiss, to let her feelings flow, grow, to not think or try to rush for a completion, to not worry if she should be touching back yet.

It was an incredible gift that he gave her.

The most exquisite lesson in lovemaking.

He gave her memories, experience, knowledge. He

gave her the world in a soft cocoon of wondrous sensations.

He took her through every emotion she could possibly imagine, made her feel every ounce of pleasure she could possibly feel. Tenderly. Reverently, with clever hands and lips, with the tips of his fingers and the stroke of his tongue.

With just the right press of his body over hers, he brought her to climax after climax. When she thought she could take it no more, he proved her wrong. When she thought she'd felt all there was to feel, he gave her more.

He kissed the tears from her eyes, sipped the perspiration from her brow, stroked the goose bumps from her thighs.

And when at last he removed his clothes and joined their bodies, gently, slowly, exquisitely, Whitney sobbed—in gratitude and in pleasure and in love.

SHE WANTED TO LIE this way forever, until the end of time. Through the window she chose a twinkling star in the velvety sky, tried to think of a wish, and couldn't settle on a single one. There were so many. Too many. And they all had to do with Dylan. All her wishes, her hopes and dreams and fantasies were wrapped up in him. He was her love, everything she needed. And she loved him with all her heart and soul, truly and deeply.

Neither had spoken after that earth-shattering experience of lovemaking. And Whitney wouldn't have known what to say anyway.

She was exhausted. Defeated by her overwhelming emotions.

They lay there, spoon fashion, her back tucked up

against his front. She felt Dylan's breathing even out, knew he was on the verge of sleep. His hand rested low on her abdomen, right over their baby. His other arm was under her, wrapped around her chest, his thumb lightly, sporadically stroking her shoulder, holding her so close, as though he expected her to disappear in a puff of smoke.

Disappearing was the furthest thing from Whitney's mind. She wanted to stay right here in his arms, would have climbed inside him if that were possible, would have stopped the world in this moment, frozen it in forever if that were possible.

But it wasn't.

She felt his breath stir her hair. Her eyes closed.

"I love you."

His words were barely a whisper. Jolted, Whitney's eyes popped open in the dark. It felt as though her heart stopped. Then it picked up, gave a deep dizzying thud. Did he feel it?

She had two choices here. She could pretend sleep—or she could pretend to misunderstand and answer him with a flippant comeback as she might have done five years ago.

But she couldn't be flippant. And five years was a long, long time. Everything had changed. Drastically.

Heartbreakingly.

Her heart stung and her throat ached at the unfairness of life, at the bittersweet twist of fate that made it impossible for her to hope.

So she did nothing, said nothing, stayed as silent as the tears that slipped from the corners of her eyes and onto the pillow.

DYLAN WOKE to the sound of the sewing machine. Birds twittered outside and the surf crashed. The sky was overcast, clouds the color of stone threatening rain.

He almost felt like that was a bad omen, that the darkness portended something he didn't want to see.

He wondered how long she'd been up, if she'd even slept. He had slept like a baby. Making love with Whitney had soothed his soul in a way he couldn't quite put a name to.

Other than love.

This was where he wanted to be.

He didn't want the outside world to intrude. But he did have obligations.

He got up, showered and dressed, then took his cellular phone out onto the deck through the sliding-glass door that exited from the bedroom. The deck ran the whole length of the back of the house. And though it would have been nicer to have warm sun-shine, there was still something very moving about a sea roiling and churning from storm clouds. The waves rose higher in their curls, the foam splashing and roaring as it broke on itself. Gulls wheeled and cried. Surfers, protected by sleek black wet suits rode their boards just beyond the breakers, watching for the perfect swell that would set them on a wild ride to shore.

Dylan wondered if Brett Coleman was one of them sitting out there like a curious crow, bobbing, glancing skyward. A jagged bolt of lightning zigzagged from the steel-gray sky to the dark waters, far enough away to not cause concern. Still, none of the surfers made a move to paddle in.

Gutsy. Then again, guys were notorious for putting

up with the elements, testing them, trying to outwit them when it came to their sports, their fun.

He flipped open his cell phone, wishing he'd taken the time to grab a cup of coffee. But then Whitney would have seen him. He wanted to be prepared when he saw her. He wanted to have his business taken care of, be in top form. He imagined she'd had plenty of time to come up with some objections.

He was going to have a time overcoming those objections.

Especially when there were so many tangled threads knotting his own life.

He punched in Cori's home phone number, hoping to catch her before she left for work. Her voice mail activated, and he hesitated. It wasn't in good form to leave another woman's phone number on your fiancée's message machine. Besides, he needed to talk to her in person. So he tried the Montgomery Beach Police Department and his frustration level nearly shot through the roof.

"Detective Spencer's off today," the sergeant said.

"Did she leave a number where she could be reached?" Dylan asked.

"I'm not at liberty to give out that information."

Great. Batting a thousand, here. "Look, is she off as in home, or off as in on assignment."

"I'm not at liberty—"

"Fine," Dylan interrupted. "Never mind."

With his gut twisting into tighter knots, he punched in Mark Forrester's mobile number.

He'd barely said two words before Forrester was blasting him. "Where the hell are you?"

Dylan sighed. *In both heaven and hell.* "I'm at Karl Delaney's beach house."

"Why?"

"I'm with Whitney."

There was silence. Telling silence. Dylan didn't try to fill it, didn't try to make excuses. The company was still in a mess, but he was still the boss. He didn't answer to anybody anymore. Well, technically...

"Why are you with Whitney Emerson?" Mark finally asked very carefully. More than an employee, Mark was a friend.

"I needed some time alone."

"Hanging out with a beautiful woman's not exactly being alone, pal."

Dylan didn't comment. He didn't want to define his relationship with Whitney, didn't want to define his feelings.

Mark, an astute man, picked up on the vibes and quickly brushed them aside. "Well, God knows nobody would begrudge you time off. You've been put through the wringer lately. However, with the stock plunging, the natives are getting restless. We lost the Acertrend account this morning."

A biggie, Dylan thought. Two million in sales a year. It would hurt. But it wouldn't ruin them. At least not by itself, and not the way this outstanding loan and balloon payment would.

"We'll work around Acertrend. There are other accounts out there."

Mark heaved an agitated sigh. "Yeah, well, all I've got to say is you better sign those merger papers the second you say 'I do' or we might as well bend over and kiss our backsides goodbye."

AS BAD OMENS WENT, that was fairly high on the scale. Pushing the sliding-glass door open, Dylan stepped into the kitchen, poured himself a cup of much needed coffee and went in search of Whitney.

Second mistake of the morning. How in the world had a beautiful twenty-four hours turned to dust this way?

She had that damned wedding dress hanging right smack in the middle of the living room, its padded hanger hooked onto a free-standing metal pole attached to a garment holder on rollers. He'd brought the thing in and put it together. If he'd known what she was going to hang on it, he would have left it in the van—or better yet, he'd have bent it into a pretzel and hidden it.

Lightning streaked the sky and thunder crashed, shaking the house. Whitney jumped, whipped around, one hand to her heart, the other covering her stomach as though to protect the baby from harm.

Either that or she was going to be sick.

He automatically moved toward her. "Are you all right?"

"Uh, yes. Startled, I guess."

He glanced at the dress. He supposed it was pretty, as wedding gowns went. He'd never really paid that much attention, hadn't thought he'd ever want to.

And he didn't. Unless it was Whitney who intended to wear it.

The rain came down in sheets as though the sky had literally opened up and somebody had turned on a faucet. Dylan checked the sliding-glass door, realized the wind wasn't blowing in their direction and left it open. The smell of rain was restful, and he needed anything remotely resembling restful to draw on here.

He had a bad feeling.

When he turned back around, that white wedding dress stared him in the face like a surrender flag.

He wouldn't surrender.

Another boom of thunder rattled the windows.

"I think the gods are trying to tell you something," she said.

"Like what?"

"Like it's bad luck to see this dress." She smoothed her hand down the satin, lifted the hem to inspect the stitches.

"You don't actually believe in that malarkey, do you?" He took a step closer, trying to gauge her mood.

She shrugged, backed up a step. A subtle move, but he noticed it nonetheless. "Uncle Karl does."

He kept coming, feeling as though he were having to sneak up on a skittish kitten, that at any minute now, she would bolt.

He hadn't known he was a patient man. He was learning quite a few new things this week about himself and what he wanted.

Carefully, slowly, he reached out, ran a fingertip down her cheek. She closed her eyes, took a deep breath. Resigned. Painful. Sad.

"What is it, Slim?"

Oh, God, the misery in her green eyes tore him up. She shook her head, didn't speak.

"Are you sick?"

"No." She cleared her throat, knocked on the pine wood coffee table. "So far so good this morning."

He set his coffee mug down, cupped her cheeks,

and pressed his lips to hers. He felt her hesitation. His gut clenched. That bad feeling was starting to annoy him.

"Maybe we should go back to bed. Maybe that's what's chased away the morning sickness."

He felt her emotional tug of war, then felt her lips curve against his. Okay, this was more like it. She was trying to back away from him, but she was losing the battle.

He didn't want to give her the opportunity to think.

"Stay right here." He gave her shoulders a squeeze.

"What?"

"Just wait." He jogged to her bedroom, snatched a jacket off the hanger, snagged a baseball cap off the shelf, then charged back into the living room.

She was still standing right where he'd told her to. He grinned. "I think we've set a record. I don't ever remember you doing something I told you to do."

She frowned. "I must still be groggy from sleep. You're confusing the daylights out of me. What did you tell me to do that I did?"

"Stay still."

"Oh. Well, don't go patting yourself on the back and feeling all dominate. I was so stunned by you running in the house, my legs were paralyzed. Purely unintentional, I assure you. Now, what in the world are you doing?"

He lifted her arms, threaded them through the sleeves of her coat, plopped the cap on her head and gave the bill a tug.

She automatically reached up and straightened it, pulled her hair through the opening in the back, using it like a ponytail holder.

And, my goodness, she was doing it again, being all docile, doing just as he said. It was going to stop.

"What in the world has gotten into you? Why are we putting on our outer wear?" Especially since he'd just teased her with the idea of going back to bed—not that she'd take him up on it.

"Because we're going to walk in the rain."

"Are you nuts? There's thunder and lightning out there."

"Not anymore."

"Well, give it a minute."

"Come on, Slim. Since when did a little thunder and lightning slow you down? It's southwest of us, anyway, and moving away instead of closer. We're not in any danger."

"Humph," was all she said. They might not be in danger from the lightning, but she was certainly in danger of his charm. She'd promised herself she would resist him, would find a way to send him on his way today.

And then he came in being all sweet and solicitous of her health, smelling like a man ought to smell and looking all cute and handsome and so damned lovable. How in the world was a sane woman supposed to resist all that?

For that matter, her sanity was debatable right now. She'd deliberately put the wedding dress in the middle of the room so he couldn't miss it. A reminder of what was at stake.

Now, in the light of day, she felt guilty for her selfishness, for making love to Dylan when he was engaged to another woman. Never mind that the engagement was more or less a forced one.

There was no way around it. He *had* to marry Cori

Spencer. And all the feelings in the world wouldn't change that.

And when he did marry her, Whitney would not, never, ever, even consider a physical relationship with him. Oh, engagements were supposed to mean something, sure, but they weren't sacred. Not like wedding vows.

So she still had until Saturday. And she might as well go for that walk in the rain. It was a lovely idea. Any time she could spend with Dylan would be a treasure.

And the fact that she was rationalizing what they had done together told her just how crazy she had become.

They stepped out onto the patio and Dylan put his arm around her shoulders, pulled her close to his side. The torrential spate of rain that had come down earlier had trickled to a gentle drizzle. The surfers weren't bothered by it. They still bobbed on their boards like a bunch of blackbirds.

Careful to negotiate the concrete steps and not slip on the wet sand that mounded on them, Whitney glanced up briefly. Her heart lurched into her mouth. For an instant she could have sworn she saw Bobby McCullaugh just beyond Brett's patio.

But what would the detective be doing lurking around the side of Brett's house? Was Bobby undercover in some sort of investigation?

She didn't want to know. And she felt really guilty. What if Cori was with him? And if not, what if he mentioned to her that he'd seen her groom coming out of another woman's house early in the morning?

She ducked from beneath Dylan's arm, skipped a

little ahead of him. He just grinned at her as though she'd challenged him to a race.

"Not this morning, Slim. This is a leisurely walk in the rain. I'm not giving you the chance to trip me again."

One more surreptitious glance over her shoulder showed that the beach was clear. Feeling calmer now that nobody was watching them—maybe she'd just imagined that the detective was there—Whitney dropped back by his side. She was being silly. She and Dylan were best friends. Anybody could vouch for their closeness, and the fact that they often held hands, raced, frolicked. It wasn't unusual for him to haul her around piggyback, for them to chase and laugh and act like a couple of fools.

The people they both knew wouldn't blink an eye.

So she satisfied her longing and reached for his hand, entwining her fingers with his.

She didn't intend to make love with him again. Last night had been a weakness. She was stronger today. But she would enjoy him, be here for him.

He was marrying a woman he didn't want to. Was forced by circumstances. He needed an ally in his corner.

Now she just had to figure out how to keep him from kissing her senseless. Because when he did that, all her good intentions would disappear in a puff of smoke.

DYLAN'S HAIR WAS WET and dripping in his eyes by the time they got back to the house. The walk had done them both good, put lots of color in Whitney's cheeks and made him feel easier, erasing that nagging sense of doom that had settled over him when he'd awoken to clouds and Mark Forrester's bad news.

But no sooner had they gotten back, stripped off their wet coats and hats, did Dylan realize that the day was indeed going to live up to its crummy beginnings.

Karl Delaney stood on the front porch of his own house, knocking on the door.

Dylan answered the summons, frowned. "Did you forget your key?"

"*Nyet.* It would not be polite to enter unannounced when I had knowledge that Whitney was here, and that you, also, were here."

"I don't recall telling you I'd be staying."

Karl's blues eyes assessed shrewdly. "I do not recall you misplacing your intelligence before."

Dylan nodded his head, conceding the round to the older man. Karl wasn't stupid. He knew the score. Hell, he'd orchestrated it, helped it along.

And he knew Dylan's heart, had known it before Dylan had had the good sense to acknowledge.

"Come in out of the rain. Whitney will be glad to see you."

"I am not so sure."

That bad feeling sat up and howled. "Why?"

Karl didn't have a chance to answer before Whitney breezed into the room.

"Uncle Karl! Is something wrong?" She kissed her uncle on the cheek, frowned at the uncomfortable expression on his face.

"I, er, was dispatched to speak with Dylan."

"Oh? Should I leave the room?"

"*Nyet.*"

When Karl used his native language, even though

it was sprinkled sporadically through his speech, it meant that he was upset or angry or uncomfortable. She waited to see which emotion ruled this morning.

"Did you have a message for me?" Dylan asked.

"In a manner of speaking. It appears that the bride's family is speculating on why the groom is keeping company with another woman when there is a wedding to take place in two days' time."

Chapter Thirteen

Whitney sank onto the sofa. Her heart thundered in her chest and her stomach roiled.

She didn't want it to end this soon. But time had just run out.

"Uncle Karl, surely the Spencers know that Dylan and I are just friends. They can ask anyone—even Cori." She refused to look at Dylan, even though she could feel his gaze boring into her. "You told them that, didn't you?"

"I did not feel it my place to get involved, my dove."

Karl studied the two young people in the room. The energy and tension here fairly shouted. Dylan was looking at Whitney as though he wanted to throttle her, or make mad passionate love to her.

Good.

Just what Karl wanted to see. These kids were meant to be together. Friends. Bah.

But Karl could put on as good an act as Whitney. He would do just a hint more meddling, a gentle push that would stir the emotions, perhaps bring things to a head. Surely the two did not plan to wait until the very day of the wedding to make a decision.

Although if they were going to speak to the bride and rectify matters, they were going to run into some difficulties.

Karl himself had thought to do a little nudging in that corner, also. It was plain as the nose on one's face where Cori Spencer's affections lay—and they weren't with Dylan Montgomery, her intended groom. It was beyond Karl why everyone was being so blessed stubborn. However, Cori Spencer was nowhere to be found.

At times that job of hers as a detective required her to go deep undercover. But would such an assignment be on deck this close to her wedding? A wedding that Karl was doing his darnedest to make sure did not take place?

"Uncle Karl," Whitney chided. "You are always getting involved and you know it. So why didn't you set Cori's parents straight? There's a billion-dollar merger hinging on this marriage. We can't let anything happen to make bad feelings."

Karl glanced sharply at Dylan. He hadn't heard of this merger, or the seriousness. Had he blundered?

"Perhaps I have overstated the urgency of the Spencers' concerns. It was a mere mention, one that I felt I should pass along should anyone care to make corrections to the situation."

Whitney felt as if her heart was ripping in two. She didn't know how much longer she could bluff, keep a smile on her face, act as though this was just a pleasant conversation, a problem easily solved. She was going to have to let Dylan go. She was going to have to *make* him let *her* go, to convince him that she didn't care enough, didn't love him deep enough. And it was going to kill her.

She was clinging to her sanity by a mere thread.

"We appreciate you letting us know, Uncle Karl."

"I'll call them," Dylan said, interrupting at last, his voice very quiet. His eyes were haunted, intense, questioning.

And focused on her.

She squirmed. She knew he could sense the change in her. Good. If he was off balance, she would have that much better chance of convincing him that she was indeed sincere, that he *had* to leave. To get on with his life.

"Well," Karl said, shifting from foot to foot. It had been a long time since he had felt so uncomfortable in one of his matchmaking, advice-giving ventures. It was in the hands of the gods now. Or up to the two kids. He had faith that they would make the right choices, straighten it out.

Surely they would.

"I'll just be on my way, then. I will have customers wondering why I have closed the door of the store."

Whitney stood, crossed the room and kissed her uncle. "I'll be in tomorrow. You shouldn't have to handle the store all by yourself."

"Ah, no, my dove. It was not my intention to interrupt your time away. You must take as long as you need to rest and recover your nerves, to make your life right. The two of you must—"

"Uncle Karl, I feel wonderful. I'll be in tomorrow."

He was losing his touch for certain. But he would leave. *Nudge only,* he reminded himself. For now, at least. Rarely did it come to the point that he had to take over and insist that people do the right thing, to

make them do the right thing. He would not like to
be the one to tell the Spencers that Whitney was
carrying Dylan's baby, that Dylan and Whitney were
in love and should be the ones getting married, not
Dylan and Cori.

But he would. There was always the part at the
wedding about speaking objections or forever holding one's peace. That would be a nasty turn of events
for sure, if it came to it, but he would make sure that
a terrible mistake did not happen with irreversible
consequences.

And in the meantime he would have to do some
thinking on this dilemma with Dylan's firm. He
hadn't known the extent of the trouble. This was not
a good thing. It would turn Gracie's life upside
down. It would also hurt Candice.

Yes, Karl would have to think long and hard about
this. And he had a mere two days to consider a path
of action.

WHEN WHITNEY SHUT the door behind Karl, she
pressed her hand to the wood jamb for a minute, took
a breath, then turned.

Dylan was still standing in the middle of the room,
a muscle twitching in his jaw.

"I don't like your mood, Whitney. I know what
you're doing."

"What am I doing? Uncle Karl needs me to help
him run the store. It's not fair to put it all off on
him." She moved across the room, keeping her distance when all the while she wanted to throw her
arms around Dylan, to hide from the world, for it to
be just the two of them. "Besides, he deserves more

free time to himself. He's made so many sacrifices for me. It's time he started living."

Dylan frowned. "He's not doing anything he doesn't want to."

"Maybe not, but I think there are things he would rather do, perhaps a relationship he'd like to renew."

"And you think you're holding him back?"

She picked up a silver thimble, pushed it on and off her finger. They were getting further away from the subject that needed to be addressed. She felt like a coward. A heartbroken coward. "I might be holding him back in certain respects. I need to pursue that big break. I'm on the verge, Dylan. As soon as I get my label recognized, picked up by a few of the high-end buyers, and have a couple of shows, Uncle Karl will rest assured that I'm on my way. He won't spend so much time worrying about me being taken care of, or fretting over my happiness. Uncle Karl knows that being a top designer is what will make me happy."

"Is that all that'll make you happy?"

"No." She put the thimble down, fussed with a pin cushion. "But it's a very big part of it."

"What about the baby? What about me?"

Giving him a smile was the hardest thing she'd ever done. "The baby will be fine. I might even design a line of baby clothes. Kind of like that drawing I did of the evening wear with the backpack—"

"What about *me*, Whitney," he repeated.

Oh, God, she was going to cry. "You're my best friend."

"Bull." He swore, raked a hand through his hair, gave a look that nearly pierced her soul. "We've gone way beyond friendship and you know it."

"Hormones," she said. Her smile slipped, trembled. Her lips stuck to her teeth.

"What the hell is the matter with you?"

She wasn't a good actress, after all. Her throat ached and her eyes stung. Her hands were shaking like palm fronds in a hurricane.

She took a breath, prayed that she could last without folding. "Dylan, there's a billion-dollar deal riding on your marriage to Cori. We've discussed this."

"And everything's changed."

"Has it? You've suddenly come up with the money to bail the company out? To save your mom's home?"

"I will. I can."

"Why should you chance it? The Spencers are offering you a sure thing. It's your dream, Dylan. I'm not going to let you sacrifice your dream."

"What's with all this talk about sacrifice?"

"It seems to be what everybody's doing lately. We've had a nice week together, Dylan. Sure, we've gone to bed together again, but you're a sexy, persuasive guy."

"That's ugly. You wanted it, too."

"Okay, so I did. But now it's time to get on with what's real. You've got a bride waiting for you. A laser design pending. A ton of families depending on you to make sure their jobs are safe. I've got Paris waiting."

"Whitney, you're having my baby."

"I know. But that doesn't change anything. I can still go to Paris. Still sew my designs. I work for myself. My baby will go where I go."

"It's my baby, too."

"Of course it is. And I'd never keep your child

from you. Don't you see, Dylan? Nothing has to change. I don't *want* it to change. For our child's sake, we've got to make a vow never to lose our closeness, but we are still better off living separate lives. You can see us whenever you like, as often as you like. It's the best of both worlds. We can still play volleyball, poker, fly kites in the sand. Our child will learn about friendship and competitiveness from us.

"I don't want our child to learn about divorce. Or bitterness. I don't want to lose what we have now. And if you look at the majority of marriages nowadays, there is the real possibility of that happening to us." Her voice escalated. Desperation clawed at her insides. Her mind was made up. He *had* to see that she was right. She had to convince him. She had to convince herself, make herself believe.

"I don't want to take that chance, Dylan. It's important to me. You've got to understand. How can I *make* you understand?" She was crying and didn't even realize it.

He stepped up to her, reached for her.

She jerked back, couldn't let him touch her. If she did, it would all be over. There was a final hurdle to clear. The toughest.

"I love you, Dylan. I love you like a friend. Nothing more. It's just not the kind of love that can guarantee us a forever after. Don't make me give up that love for the baby's sake. He or she will thank us for remaining close."

"Why are you so certain it would all turn rotten?"

Oh, she wasn't. But it was the only flimsy excuse she could come up with. And since it was, she had to make sure she convinced him. *Don't cry. Don't scream. Hold it together.*

"I told you I'm not certain. But I don't want to take a chance. I don't want to wreck your dream, Dylan. And if you stayed with me that could happen."

She touched him then, poured steel into her backbone, forced her hand to be steady. "Please, Dylan. I don't ask much of you, but I'm asking you this. Please. Leave, get on with your life. Marry Cori. Build your dream, your lasers. Save your family's estate."

The raw look in his eyes ripped her in two. Her insides were frozen. Those tears wouldn't be dammed. They slid down her cheeks.

"Please, Dylan. Don't make me hurt you. Don't hurt me. Don't change what's between us. Please go."

He didn't say a word. He leaned down, pressed his lips to her temple as he'd done so very many times in their lives.

As a friend.

As if nothing had ever changed between them.

Oh, my God, she'd convinced him. The urge to take it all back was huge. She resisted.

He took a breath. "I love you, Slim."

She swallowed, blinked, wiped the tears off her cheek, gave a watery laugh. "I know. And I love you, too, buddy."

"No, I mean—"

She quickly put her fingers over his lips. "Come on, get going," she interrupted. "You've got a wedding to think about, a merger to finalize. I've got sewing to do and designs to create. While you're on your honeymoon someplace, I'll be in Paris convincing folks that I'm the next rising star and they'd better sit up and take notice.''

"I'm not going on a honeymoon." He took her fingers in his, moved them from his lips to his chest, right over his heart. "That's already been agreed on. Cori is busy, so am I."

"Shame on you." She felt his heavy heartbeat, saw the frustration in his velvety brown eyes. "But you can always take one later. Hey, you can stop over in Paris."

"Damn it, Whitney."

She stepped away, wrapped her arms around her middle. She couldn't hold on much longer. "Go, Dylan. You're not going to change my mind. And I'm not going to say something that will hurt you. Please go."

The space between them might as well have been a deep crevice filled with boiling lava, uncrossable. They stood on opposite edges, sharing a glance, unable to bridge the gap, to make it right. Life was out of control.

Out of *their* control.

And that made it hurt all the worse.

"Be happy, Dylan," she whispered.

He turned, then, without a word, and strode out the door. She wanted to run after him, to call him back, to make him tell her what that last enigmatic look had meant. But she couldn't, wouldn't.

She heard the clank of the automatic garage door as it rose, listened to the Porsche roar to life, peel out, the tires squealing on the concrete. There would be black rubber tracks down the driveway.

When she could no longer hear the engine, she

sank onto the couch, curled into herself, feeling numb, in a daze, stunned.

She'd just sent the man she loved into the arms of another woman. A woman she wished she could hate, but couldn't.

And though Whitney had told Dylan she would see him at the wedding, that just wasn't going to happen. She couldn't—wouldn't—be able to stand the pain. She wasn't that much of a masochist. She would deliver the dress, and then...well, then she would try to put the pieces of her broken heart back together, a rend that she'd caused herself, couldn't blame on Dylan or anybody else.

She rested a protective hand over her abdomen. There was one consolation in this whole miserable mess, a silver lining. She knew Dylan Montgomery better than anyone else. She would be able to answer any questions her child might have about his father...

Except one, she realized.

The one about why she'd let him walk out of their lives.

Would her child understand her sacrifice?

Her sacrifice for love?

DYLAN PRESSED on the accelerator and just drove. Aimlessly. By rote. He didn't know where he was going, had no concept of the miles he'd traveled. He only had a vague idea that he was heading south. When he ended up almost at the state line, he realized he'd come too far. His mind was empty, yet busy, if that were possible.

And at the root of everything was Whitney. He loved her. Truly. Madly. Deeply.

There was no way in the world he could marry

someone else. God, the responsibilities of his decisions were phenomenal. What about his mother? His sister? The jobs at stake? All the families of his employees? Their health benefits would come to an end. Their children's braces wouldn't get paid for. Long-planned vacations would be canceled; that special, coveted anniversary ring would be returned.

Oh, Dylan could rebuild, perhaps make it to a point where he could rehire everyone, but would it be too late for some? Would lives be irreparably ruined?

The sun had long since set and the sky was a deep indigo. He was hungry and tired, his mind and body feeling abused.

He picked up the car phone, punched in Cori Spencer's number once more. He'd been trying for hours—days actually—to get in touch with her, but she was not answering. He'd known she was busy. Hell, this whole wedding was supposed to have taken place on the fly—just a couple of hours off to say a few words in front of a judge so William Spencer would have a legal piece of paper to press forward with the merger. Then Cori's mother had gotten involved and things had gone downhill and horribly wrong from there.

Then again, if there hadn't been such a hullabaloo, might he have married quietly without seeing Whitney again? Without finding out about the baby? Without admitting and acknowledging how deep his feelings ran? How deeply they'd always ran?

Cori's answering matching came on, her sweet, no-nonsense voice stating that nobody was available to answer the call. They were both caught in a bad place. He knew Cori didn't love him. She had her own reasons for agreeing to the wedding. He wasn't certain what they were. He needed to find out, to see if there was a way around it.

God, what a mess. Lives touched, ruined perhaps. And though Cori's feelings weren't engaged, would not marrying him have consequences for her, too?

He left a message, recited all of his phone numbers so she could get in touch with him. He knew he should get a hotel room, get some rest, or at least pull over to the side of the road and close his eyes for a few minutes.

But there wasn't time. The road signs told him it would take nearly a full day to get back to Montgomery Beach.

So he pulled off the nearest freeway ramp, and got back on in the opposite direction.

Heading home.

Home to Whitney.

He nearly made it back. He reached up to rub his eyes. Just that split second that he slid his weary eyes off the road was all it took for disaster to happen.

A flash of red. An older sedan. Illegal left turn.

Dylan slammed on the brakes, might have shut his eyes.

He heard the scream of tires skidding on asphalt, felt the muscles in his legs and arms bulge as he braced, pressed, prayed.

He jerked the wheel, helplessly sliding toward destruction, out of control. At the last minute, in one split second of clarity, he released the brake and stomped down hard on the gas. The powerful engine responded, and the rear end yanked around, shooting the Porsche out of the skid, giving him much needed traction to steer out of harm's way, missing the other idiot by mere paint chips.

And he would have made it just fine.

But he was tired. And his reflexes weren't as good as he'd thought.

He overcorrected on that last maneuver, put the car into a spin. The tires hit the curb, popped like a balloon stuck with a pin, then hurtled the frame against the light pole.

The seat belt jerked against his chest and the air bag exploded in his face.

Dylan saw a wall of white, and then black.

And into the darkness he said one word. "Whitney."

IT WAS LATE Friday night. Whitney hadn't heard from Dylan since he'd left her house yesterday. Cori Spencer's wedding dress was finished, as best as Whitney could do it. Now there was just the final fitting to be conducted. Doing it at nine o'clock at night was certainly pushing it. If the seams were still not right, Whitney would be up until dawn fixing them. But Cori was busy these days.

And that worried Whitney.

What kind of a marriage would Cori and Dylan have? If neither could make the time to talk, to see one another, to even schedule and enjoy a wedding, what kind of life would that be?

She had the lights on in the tux shop—she'd asked Cori to come here rather than the bridal shop. Leena's responsibility was over now.

A soft knock on the glass. Whitney went to let in the detective.

She glanced around. "Your partner's not with you?"

Amazingly enough, Cori Spencer blushed. "No, we're off for the night."

"Okay. You can change in the dressing room back there. And, Cori?" The other woman paused on her way to the curtained area. "Strip this time, would you?" Cori gave a wave and disappeared into the cubicle.

Where was the joy? The giddiness associated with weddings? This was purely depressing.

But, oh, she looked like an absolute dream in that dress, Whitney admitted several minutes later.

Truly stunning.

"Step on the pedestal," Whitney said softly, feeling that only a hushed voice would do in this instance. Cori Spencer reminded her a bit of the late Princess of Wales. Short blond hair falling softly around her ears, a diamond tiara resting at her crown holding a multilayered veil. Australian satin and lace and pearls and crystal. A train that fanned like a regal robe trailed a good twelve feet behind her.

Whitney tugged and measured and decided she was happy with the length. She'd done a fine job considering she'd been calculating based on combat boots. The satin pumps Cori now wore were more like it.

She glanced up at the other woman. The preoccupied, *sad* woman. Cori must have felt the stillness. She looked down. Their eyes met. Woman to woman. Here, with the lights low and no one to hear, they could speak their hearts.

Or speak around them.

"Do you love him?" Whitney asked past the lump in her throat.

"Honestly?"

"Honestly."

"Then, no. I like him. I respect him. And he was my father's choice. Daddy's adamant about this merger, these lasers Dylan's so excited about. Anyway…I've been a disappointment to Daddy. He's never approved of my work or my ideas. We've butted heads all my life. And I truly have wanted it to be otherwise. I've wished since I was a little girl that I could be his princess, that I could make him happy, that he would approve, that I could somehow make up for my little brother's death."

Whitney's hands went still. Oh, this was tough. And so emotional.

"I know it sounds really dumb and archaic and silly to you," Cori continued, "but it's important to me. When I agreed to the marriage, for the first time in my life I'd done something that he actually approved of. He beamed, Whitney. I've never seen him beam before—not at me." There were tears in Cori's eyes. "I've let him down before, disappointed him. I can't do it again."

Whitney nodded. The sadness was overwhelming. For both of them. All of them. The ball was rolling and to stop it would have far-reaching consequences.

She wondered if Randolph Montgomery was chuckling from his grave over in Dillard's cemetery. After all, he was getting just what he wanted. A marriage merger between his son and Cori Spencer.

And just as when he was alive, all the concerned parties were not happy about it, were feeling twisted inside out, yet were swept along regardless.

And Dylan was caught up in it most of all. Although Whitney would rather kiss a snake than go to that wedding, she knew she'd have to. He needed her in his corner.

Because she knew Dylan. Honor and integrity were part of him. Once he said those vows, he would not compromise them. Never mind that his back was to the wall. He wouldn't make excuses. He would sacrifice. And he would uphold those vows.

She would have to be at that wedding tomorrow. To show her support, her love. To let him know that she understood. That it would be okay. That he would still be their baby's father. That he would still be in their lives.

That she would never expect him to break the vows he would make. That she would always be his friend. His port in the rocky storms. His confidant.

His friend.

Chapter Fourteen

The Porsche was a mess, but Dylan was lucky. Other than burns on his arms from the air bag, a bruise across his chest from the seat belt, and four stitches in his eyebrow from his head hitting the side window, he was in one piece.

"I know it's the job of the best man to make sure the groom gets to the church on time, but we usually like to do our job with a little less drama," Jack O'Connor commented. He leaned against the wall of the curtained cubical in the emergency room, holding out a shirt.

Dylan accepted the shirt and pushed his arms through the sleeves. He wasn't in the mood to talk right now. He had a lot to do and very little time to do it in. And he was still so damned confused, still felt so damned responsible for everybody.

A legacy left to him by his father. Even now, he could hear the echo of his father's voice. *You'll do the right thing, son. It's expected of you. You know your place. Do as I would do.*

God, he didn't want to do as his father would have done. He was so tired of living in that shadow.

Life was too damned short. He'd realized that with

sparkling clarity the instant the air bag had deployed like a shotgun blast in his face.

"Thanks for coming, Jack."

"Anytime, buddy. You know that."

"Yeah." But there was a preoccupation on Jack's part. O'Connor was a good friend, but it was different than what Dylan shared with Whitney—besides the obvious distinction that Jack was a guy. And Jack seemed to have his own set of problems on his mind. God knows the man had a lot on his plate. Raising a boy on his own, relocating. He was a millionaire, everything he touched turning to gold. Half the time he didn't even try to make money. It just multiplied.

Dylan considered asking him for a loan.

He couldn't do it. Not yet anyway. Pride was a nasty thing, sure, but it was there nonetheless.

Besides, he needed some answers. Some information. Then he would have a point to go from.

"So, where to?" Jack asked as they walked through the automatic emergency room door into the buttery California sunshine.

"The estate. I need to talk to my mom."

"Sure thing."

Dylan closed his eyes and slouched in the leather seat of the Suburban, never saying a word during the twenty-mile trip to the Montgomery estate. And other than a couple glances in his direction, Jack didn't push, respected the need for silence.

SHE WAS PLAYING the piano again. Dressed in her mother-of-the-groom dress. Pretty, Dylan noted. Grace Montgomery didn't look fifty-nine, could have passed for a much younger woman. Her skin was clear, her ash-blond hair swept up off her neck, discreet diamonds winking at her ears.

She'd taken off her wedding ring soon after his father's death, and in its place wore a tasteful pearl clustered in diamonds. She was small and trim, delicate in stature, yet strong of character. She could be oh-so-correct when the occasion called for it.

But she was a mother first and always. Dylan had always known that, felt secure in that knowledge.

He moved into the room, slipped in beside her on the piano bench. "Hey, beautiful."

Her lips curved, her fingers halted over the keys. She turned to him, and her expression of welcome turned to one of horror, the kind of horror only a mother could express with such feeling.

"Dylan, oh, my God, what happened?" She reached for his face, her fingers cool and soothing, dancing over his cheek, hovering over his stitches.

"I'm fine, Mom. The Porsche and I had a tangle with a light pole."

"Oh, darling, I've told you your racing around in that machine was going to get you in trouble."

"Actually, it was an idiot in a sedan making an illegal left turn that got me in trouble."

"Oh." She smiled, pressed a kiss to his hurt cheek. Just as she'd done so many times when he was a boy. Her kisses could always make it better.

He felt his eyes burn, his throat close. Ah, hell, he wasn't going to cry in front of his mother. He was the one who was supposed to be taking care here, protecting, making everything right. He was the one she would ultimately lean on.

Or was he? If he really looked, he would see the strength that radiated out of those contemplative blue eyes. The women in the family were the strong ones, he realized, the ones with the backbone. And God knows his mother had had a rough time of it. She'd had to be so many things to so many people, wore a multitude of hats, held down a multitude of jobs. Having money had eased some of the burdens, but not all.

The biggest burden had been the demands of Randolph Montgomery, so many of them unreasonable. And damn it, even the unreasonable ones were met. They all jumped through hoops.

"What is it, darling?"

He turned his eyes to the ceiling. "You always could read me. I'm confused, Mom."

"I can see that. Talk to me, son."

He looked at Grace Montgomery. "Why did you stay with him?"

She looked away.

"Were you happy?"

"I was happy with you and Candy," she said softly, without hesitation.

The words stung him. "We're still living in Dad's shadow, aren't we?"

"It's a heavy shadow."

"Whitney's pregnant."

Grace's china-blue eyes fired with emotion—the censor of a mother who knows her son's too old to scold, the elation of a grandmother, the gentleness of a friend. "Yours?"

"Yes."

"Then what in the world is this Spencer wedding about, son?"

He sucked in a breath and put his arm around his mother's shoulders. "The company's in a mess. Dad screwed up. I'm trying to hold on to the business, to hold on to your house.''

''My... Dylan Montgomery, I could smack you. Are you sitting here telling me you're marrying a woman you don't love so I can still live in this monster of a house?''

''It's been your home for thirty-five years. Your memories are here.''

''My memories are in videos and photos, too. I don't need this huge place. It was your father's pride and joy, not mine. Mine was you children. Just you kids. That's all. Let it go, Dylan. For God's sake, call it off and let it all go.''

She was right. They were playing to Randolph's tune. He'd been doing it for thirty-two years. It was time it stopped. And it would stop with him.

''I need to talk to Cori. I haven't been able to get in touch with her.''

''That's odd. I saw her at the pier festival.''

''You were at the pier festival?'' Had she seen him with Whitney?

''Yes. And I saw Cori there with Bobby Mc-Cullaugh.''

''He's her partner. They were probably working.'' And had *they* seen him with Whitney? Oh, that wouldn't be a nice way for Cori to find out his feelings. It would be really rotten.

''They didn't look like just partners to me.''

That got Dylan's attention. ''What do you mean?''

WHITNEY WAS VIOLENTLY sick that morning. It looked as though she was going to have a legitimate excuse for missing the wedding after all. She couldn't get her head out of the toilet long enough to get dressed.

Then the baby seemed to hear her thoughts and gave her a reprieve.

"Well, thanks a lot, sweetheart. You're braver than I if you want to go see your daddy get married." She fixed her hair, pulled on a pair of panty hose, then hooked her bra and spritzed on her signature scent of white gardenia, attending to her toiletry by rote.

"Though in truth he really does need a friend there. He's in a mess right now with the business. We need to be there to support him, to make sure he feels secure in what he's doing, to give our blessings."

She put her hand over her tummy. "I promise I'll make sure you never feel a loss because of this marriage, sweetie. He's opening a branch of his company here in town. He'll come and see you all the time. We'll be like a family, he will just live with Cori, that's all. And you'll like her. She's cute, and she's a police detective, so she can keep the bad guys from our town and you'll always be safe."

She took a lavender skirt and camisole out of the closet, put it on, and had her black platform shoes buckled on her feet before she realized this was the same outfit she'd worn that night three months ago.

The night she and Dylan had gone to Hank's.

The night they'd made love...created a baby.

She turned sideways, looked at her reflection in the dresser mirror. Her stomach pooched against the clingy fabric. The shimmery silk shantung blazer would hide that little secret, she realized.

And it was going to have to do, or else she'd be

late. If she took the time to make up her mind about another outfit, she'd miss the whole darn wedding—which might not be a bad idea.

No, she chided herself. She'd decided to go to the thing and that was all there was to it.

The doorbell rang and she took a breath. Probably Uncle Karl, not trusting her to come on her own.

Well, he'd always been her strength, her reminder to square her shoulders and keep her chin up. She imagined she'd need some of his gentle coaching before the day was over.

She opened the door and frowned.

Two uniformed police officers stood on her porch. Her heartbeat shot into adrenaline-pumping overdrive, making her dizzy. For a law abiding citizen such as herself, police officers at the door meant an accident or tragedy.

Before she could form the dreaded question, the young officer spoke.

"Whitney Emerson?"

"Yes." Her voice trembled. Terror turned into outrage in a millisecond when a pair of shiny handcuffs appeared in the other officer's hands.

She frowned. "What—" A hand gripped her arm, very gently, to be sure. The cuffs clinked and snicked as the lock shot home. "What are you doing?"

"You're to come with us."

"I'm not going anywhere with you! Are you accusing me of a crime?"

The men shared a smile. Whitney's insides began to boil. "Well?" she demanded. "What is this all about." She had a wedding to get to, a friend to bolster.

The maddening officers turned mute as they

walked her to the squad car and carefully handed her into the back seat, making sure she didn't bump her head. She was tempted to kick them in the shins, but didn't want to push things.

"I'm entitled to a phone call, surely."

"No problem. As soon as we get there."

"Where is 'there'?"

They didn't speak. And with frustration clawing at her, she gave up trying to wheedle anything out of them.

She recognized the route they took—it was only five blocks from her house. They were going to the church.

The church that was located in the corner of the courtyard, right by the tux shop.

The church where her best friend was getting married.

Well, honestly, she thought in a bit of a huff. There might have been some worry as to whether or not she'd truly show up, but wasn't being stuffed into a squad car and delivered in handcuffs a bit much? And did Dylan all of a sudden have pull with the police department now that he was marrying one of its own?

The officers helped her out of the car. She raised a brow, held her shackled hands in front of her. "Is this necessary? I'm here. You've obviously done your job. Shouldn't you take these off now?"

"Can't. They're not ours."

Whitney started to ask, decided against it. She was having a nightmare and was wide awake. Either that or she'd gone off the deep end, lost every shred of her sanity, and somebody had forgotten to tell her about it.

The young officer tried to take her arm to steer her. She jerked away from his hold. She would walk under her own steam, thank you very much. After all, being at this church was a little like going to a firing squad. She'd do the dead man's walk with her head held high and...

Oh, for God's sake, she was getting way too dramatic here. Definitely going down for the last count.

"Uh, Ms. Emerson?"

She slowed, looked over her shoulder. "Yes?"

"This way." Rather than touch her, the officers flanked her, herded her like a couple of sheep dogs toward the hotel.

Thank goodness they didn't march her through the courtyard for all and sundry to see. As it was, there were several hotel guests who stopped to stare as though she were a criminal. For crying out loud.

They entered through the back, mounted a flight of stairs. A quick knock on a closed door.

Sure enough, Cori Spencer opened the door. She wore a wraparound silk robe in glossy ivory. Bridal ivory. Her short blond hair was teased and sprayed, a few wispy bangs falling across her brow. She didn't have on any makeup and her nails weren't painted. Her legs were bare of nylons, her toes unadorned by polish. The woman was going to be late for her own ceremony.

Cori smiled. "Thanks, guys," she said to the officers, who were even now backing away from the door.

Whitney stopped her perusal of Cori Spencer's toes and looked up. "Well, this is certainly going to the extreme. I appreciate the escort and all, but a limo would have caused less of a stir with my neighbors and…'' Her words trailed off when she glanced over Cori's shoulder.

She forgot about the handcuffs binding her wrists, about the curtains that had twitched as the officers had led her out the door and into their squad car. Forgot about Cori's state of dress or undress.

Dylan was rising from a rose damask chair in the corner—and he *was* dressed. In a tuxedo. For his wedding.

What in the world was going on? And…

''Oh, God, Dylan, what happened to your face?''

Forgetting the bride, she rushed across the room, raised her hands, annoyed at the hindrance of steel bracelets, and touched his swelling cheek.

That boyish smile and dimples flashed when he saw the handcuffs. ''I'm fine, Slim. The Porsche'll be in the shop for a while, though.''

''Screw the Porsche. Are you sure you're okay? Look, you've got stitches!''

''I know. I feel them. The drugs are wearing off.''

''Don't be flippant. Sit down. Why are you standing? Why aren't you in the hospital? Why aren't—''

To her everlasting horror and astonishment, he stopped her flow of words with his lips.

Whitney shrieked, leaped back. ''Oh, my God.'' She didn't want to look at Cori. ''Is there a gun aimed at my back?'' she whispered.

Dylan laughed. ''Uh, Cori, could you do something with these cuffs?''

Unable to put it off, Whitney turned, ready to effusively apologize to the other woman, to assure her that this would never, *ever* happen again. She'd move to Siberia if she had to.

But Cori's expression, though preoccupied, was

not angry. There wasn't a gun in sight. There was, thankfully, a key.

Whitney held out her hands. "Yes, if you'll just slip these off I'll get out of here and leave the two of you to, um…" She watched as Cori inserted a little bitty key into the cuffs. She really needed to explain that unfortunate display. "Uh, please don't pay any attention to that, uh, kiss. I've known Dylan since we were kids and…what the *devil* are you doing?"

The cuffs snicked apart and snapped again, right to the carved footboard of the raised platform bed. Stunned, Whitney's gaze touched on several things in the room, the deep rose settee, the sheer fabrics of canopies and drapes, the antique dressing tables. Then they came back to Cori. Was the woman mad?

Obviously yes. Cori Spencer turned, handed the key to Dylan, kissed him gently, *platonically* on the cheek. "Do us all a favor, Dylan, and straighten out your life."

Before Whitney could even close her astonished mouth, Cori was gone.

"Oh, no. Quick, Dylan, uncuff me then go after her. You can explain—"

He was shaking his head.

She wanted to whack him. To her horror, tears were welling in her throat. These crazy emotions were wearing old. "Don't be an idiot. There's a billion-dollar deal riding on today."

"Not anymore."

She went deadly still, utterly quiet. Her heart thudded. She wondered if he could hear it. He took a step closer. She was trapped. She couldn't evade.

"What do you mean, 'not anymore'? Oh, Dylan,

what have you done? Please don't tell me you've sacrificed your dream.''

''No,'' he said softly, so softly it made her heart ache. ''I haven't sacrificed my dream.'' His lips brushed her temple. ''*You* are my dream.''

The damned tears slipped right down her cheeks. With her free hand she tried to wipe them. Dylan's fingers beat her to the task.

And, oh, they were gentle.

''The company, Dylan.''

''The company's fine. I talked to Spencer, told him I wanted out. As it turns out, he wanted a marriage of our corporate technology more than he wanted a son-in-law. But it looks like he's going to get a son-in-law in the bargain anyway.''

Just when she'd started to hope, her stomach did a leap. ''But I thought you said—''

''Cori's in love with her partner, Bobby Mc-Cullaugh.''

''Oh.''

He grinned, ran a finger down her cheek. ''Just 'oh,' Slim?''

Her eyes narrowed, and she sniffed. Butterflies were winging through her stomach. Her emotions were on such a roller coaster she was feeling about as dizzy as a termite in a yo-yo.

But it was a thrilling sort of vertigo.

''What did you want me to say?''

''How about that you love me and can't live without me?''

Her smile was slow and sassy. The world was hers now.

Dylan was hers.

"Now, why would I say something like that? Your ego's too huge as it is."

"Not around you, it's not. Will we always have this competitiveness?"

"Always."

"There's a promise I'll have from you, though."

"What's that?"

"No more sacrifices. You were doing that for me, weren't you? Sacrificing."

She started to look away. He gently caught her chin. "You were sacrificing because you love me, weren't you? Because you *really* love me."

"Maybe."

He shook his head, his velvety brown eyes filled with amused indulgence. "One thing I'll say, our marriage is never going to be dull."

She cocked a brow. Oh, the man was so darn cute and he knew it. And he was the love of her life. But she had to get in the last word. What was it Uncle Karl always said? "Start as you intend to continue."

But somebody knocked on the door.

"Come in," Dylan said, raising his voice.

Whitney rolled her eyes, whispered fiercely. "For crying out loud, Dylan, I'm handcuffed to the bed!"

"And a good place to be if you ask me." He looked up. "Help you with something, Mc-Cullaugh?"

Bobby McCullaugh was removing his tasteful gray tie. Uncle Karl was standing right behind the detective. "Uh, Mrs. Spencer is insisting my suit's not right. She wants the groom in a tux."

"The groom?" Whitney echoed, confused.

"Yes," Karl chimed in. "Isn't it just wonderful how all has worked out so splendidly? There are preparations and caterers and a priest waiting to marry a couple. A wedding license discretely arranged.'' Karl stroked his mustache, tugged at his cuffs, bobbed his head in approval. ''The guests are arriving. And at last—though you've all cut it a bit closer than I'd have liked—at last, the parties are somewhat matched. Not all of you, mind you, but we have an excellent start.''

Who wasn't matched? Whitney wondered. But she didn't have a chance to voice the question. Karl ushered Bobby into the room, helping him slip the suit off his broad shoulders. Her uncle spared a glance at the handcuffs, never even batted an eye or changed expression.

''Nice jewelry, my dove. Now, Dylan, if you will kindly remove your jacket, we will exchange and get the proper groom started down the aisle.''

''There's still going to be a wedding?'' Whitney asked.

''Of course. It would be a crime to waste all these preparations. And this young man being in law enforcement is certainly against crime. There,'' Karl announced. ''The fit is as fine as if I'd tailored it specifically for you.'' He looked down at Bobby's black trousers. ''Those will do nicely. Carry on, you two,'' he said, looking at Dylan. ''But do not dally too long that you miss the ceremony. There will certainly be confusion and explanations needing to be handed out. Your presence will put an ease to a great deal of the speculation. I always say, the visual or the written is much more powerful and effective than the spoken.''

And with that sly reference to his notes and his roundabout way of taking credit for happy romances,

Karl ushered a nervous Bobby McCullaugh out of the room.

Whitney's head was spinning and her insides were tickling. She laughed, feeling on top of the world.

Dylan would get his laser technology. The Montgomery business and estate would be safe. Cori Spencer was marrying the man she truly loved. There was no reason why Whitney couldn't act on her own feelings, on her own love, to make her own fantasies a reality, to wrap them up with a shiny bow.

"Uncle Karl has struck again," she said, smiling.

"Looks like." His lips caressed the corner of her mouth, her cheek, her neck. Chills feathered her skin.

"Uh, Dylan?"

"Mmm?" His clever tongue was doing something incredible to her ear.

"Did I hear you mention something about marriage?"

"There wasn't any 'mention' about it, Slim. We *are* getting married."

"I gotta tell you, pal, that kind of order is not endearing you to me."

He pulled back, looked at her, a sparkle in his brown eyes. He knew her so well. "We going to arm wrestle?"

"If you don't do this right, we will."

"Do you love me?"

"More than anything."

"And I love you," he said softly. "And, since I'm going to be a daddy, I figure you really ought to make an honest man out of me."

"You're a hard guy to resist, Dylan Montgomery.

I think you better use that key and get me loose from these cuffs. There's a proper way to propose to the mother of your child, and I aim to have you do it right.''

HARLEQUIN®

A M E R I C A N ◆ R O M A N C E®

Which cowboy will become the first daddy in Cactus, Texas?

Cal, Spence, Tuck and Mac have to beware!
Their moms want grandchildren—and these
conniving matchmakers will stop at
nothing to turn their cowboy
sons into family men.

**Judy Christenberry's
4 TOTS FOR 4 TEXANS
is another winner!**

ONE HOT DADDY-TO-BE?
#773, May 1999

SURPRISE—YOU'RE A DADDY!
#777, June 1999

DADDY UNKNOWN
#781, July 1999

THE LAST STUBBORN COWBOY
#785, August 1999

4 TOTS for 4 TEXANS

Available wherever Harlequin books are sold.

HARLEQUIN®
Makes any time special™

Look us up on-line at: http://www.romance.net

HAR4TF4T

If you enjoyed what you just read,
then we've got an offer you can't resist!

Take 2 bestselling
love stories FREE!
Plus get a FREE surprise gift!

HARLEQUIN®

AMERICAN ◆ ROMANCE®

COMING NEXT MONTH

#773 ONE HOT DADDY-TO-BE? by Judy Christenberry
4 Tots for 4 Texans
Nothing is more important for four elderly mothers of Cactus, Texas, than making their sons fathers. They're not even above a little bet...so the baby race is on! Bachelor #1, Cal Baxter, never knew he'd one day be looking at his childhood friend Jessica Hoya as a prospective mother of his child...but he never knew how determined his mother could be!

#774 THE LAST TWO BACHELORS by Linda Randall Wisdom
Delaney's Grooms
"You've just seen your new mother." The prophetic note that ring bearer Patric pulls out of his tux pocket tells him he and his dad, Jack O'Connor, have a prospect for a new wife and mom...but how could that be, when she's the beautiful woman trying on a wedding gown?

#775 THE ACCIDENTAL MRS. MacKENZIE by Bonnie K. Winn
Brynn Magee had imagined herself to be Douglas MacKenzie's bride for months. But when his family suddenly mistakes her for his real-life bride, she realizes she's in love with Matt MacKenzie—the "groom's" brother!

#776 FATHER IN TRAINING by Mollie Molay
New Arrivals
It was one of those things: a moonlit night, an incredibly sexy guy, music in the background. Before she knew what happened, Abby Carson was in the arms of the man she'd been wishing for all her life. But now, was Jeff Logan ready to be a daddy?

Look us up on-line at: http://www.romance.net